W9-AGJ-247

THE HAUNTED LAGOON

Louise and Jean Dana stare unbelievingly through the swirling mists in an isolated lagoon. Floating in mid-air is a full-rigged sailing ship! A moment later it vanishes.

Never before have the Danas encountered so eerie and challenging a mystery. To find the solution, they must locate a former sea captain who mysteriously disappeared from Chincoteague Island off the Virginia coast. During their search of the neighboring islands, the two young sleuths are thwarted by a sinister enemy who resorts to desperate measures to prevent them from unearthing the truth.

Readers will share many thrilling adventures with the Danas as the young detectives and their friends pursue the baffling trail of clues that leads them to pirate treasure and a startling climax.

"He thinks we're trying to take the colt!"
Louise cried out.

The *Dana Girls* Mystery Stories

THE HAUNTED LAGOON

By Carolyn Keene

GROSSET & DUNLAP
A National General Company
Publishers   *New York*

Dedicated to Mr. and Mrs. Leo B. Wolfe and to Mr. Nat Steelman in appreciation of their help to the author during her research visit to the Island. With the permission of these kind people, their names have been used in the book.

PRINTED IN THE UNITED STATES OF AMERICA

CONTENTS

CHAPTER I

The *Sea Ghost*

"PIRATE treasure!" cried Jean Dana excitedly. The slender, blond girl was taking a ship-to-shore telephone call in her stateroom aboard the steamship *Balaska*.

"Yes, Jean," said Chris Barton, who was calling from the United States. "Ken, Ronny, and I are going down to Chincoteague Island and try to dig up treasure buried near there in 1758 by the old pirate, Charles Wilson."

"But, Chris, that was a long time ago," Jean remarked. "Surely somebody has already found it."

"We've been reading a lot about the place, and we think the treasure is still there," Chris insisted. "Jean, come help us look for it. Wouldn't you like to have a pocketful of pirate gold?"

"Of course! It does sound intriguing!"

"Then all you have to do is accept the invitation we heard you received from Doris' parents to visit them at Chincoteague."

At that moment Ken Scott took the phone from Chris Barton and asked to speak to Jean's brunette, seventeen-year-old sister. "You girls must come," he told Louise. "Chincoteague's a very interesting place—there are wild ponies and a rocket base—besides the buried treasure."

Louise chuckled. "I don't see how we can resist! Jean and I will ask Aunt Harriet about the trip. We haven't had a chance as yet—the Harlands phoned us from Virginia just a few minutes before you called."

Miss Harriet Dana and her brother Ned, captain of the *Balaska*, had brought up their nieces since the death of the girls' parents. Aunt Harriet, the two girls, and their Starhurst School chums, Doris Harland and Evelyn Starr, had been on an extensive trip in Europe. Now it was early September and nearly time for them to return to Starhurst School. Louise was entering her senior year, while Jean would be a junior.

"Before we sign off," said Ken to Louise, "Ronny wants to speak to Doris. Well, I'll say good-by now. Be seeing you in Chincoteague in a few days!"

While Doris talked to Ronny, the Danas and Evelyn whispered excitedly about the invitation. "I simply can't go," said Evelyn disappointedly. "I promised my brother I'd be home to help him attend to some very important family business."

"Oh, that's a shame, Evelyn."

When Doris heard it, she agreed. "My parents will be so disappointed," she said. "But let's find Aunt Harriet and ask her about you Danas going to Chincoteague with me."

The four girls hurried to Miss Dana's stateroom next door. She was busy packing in anticipation of their arrival in New York the following day.

"I heard your phone ring," she said, smiling. "Who was calling?" Aunt Harriet had a sweet, gentle expression, and her deep affection for her nieces was evident as she looked at them.

Their eyes dancing with excitement, Louise, Jean, and Doris told her about the Harlands' invitation to Aunt Harriet and the girls and the call from Chris and Ken urging them to accept it.

Doris broke in, "Oh, please accept the invitation, Miss Dana. You were so wonderful to me in Europe, and Mother and Dad want to show their appreciation in this way." Doris added that the Danas could fly with her by chartered plane from New York, and her parents would meet them.

Aunt Harriet smiled. "You're very persuasive, Doris. Unfortunately, I won't be able to go myself, and Louise and Jean must arrive home in plenty of time to get ready for school. But I wouldn't want to keep them from locating pirate treasure—"

"Oh, you're such a dear!" Louise cried.

Jean, planting a resounding kiss on her aunt's cheek, added, "There's not so nice an aunt in the whole world as you!"

The girls soon hurried off to their two staterooms to pack. Louise and Jean had just finished when they heard a knock on the door.

"Come in!" Jean sang out.

The door was opened by a very attractive English girl, Kim Honeywell, whom they had met on the ship. Kim was about four years older than Louise.

"Excuse my intruding like this," she said, "but I overheard you say you're going to Chincoteague. My mother and I are traveling there also."

"Oh, wonderful, Kim!" Louise smiled. "We'll see you at the island. Where are you staying?"

"The Channel Bass Hotel."

"Oh, that's where we'll be," Jean told her. "We're flying down from New York tomorrow."

Kim Honeywell said that she and her mother planned to remain in New York a few days, then fly to Salisbury, Maryland. From there they would have to hire a cab to drive them the forty-five miles to Chincoteague.

"Maybe we could rent a car and meet you," Jean offered. "When you're ready to leave New York, why don't you give us a ring?"

"That's very kind of you indeed," said Kim. "It would be a jolly ride. I'll talk it over with Mother."

"How do you happen to be going to Chincoteague?" Louise asked. "It isn't a usual tourist spot."

Kim sat down on the edge of Jean's bunk. "We

have a rather unusual reason for going there. It's a strange story. I know you girls like mysteries. Would you care to hear about this one?"

"Oh, yes!" the sisters chorused.

Louise and Jean, from the time they had solved their first case, *Mystery of the Stone Tiger*, to their latest adventure, uncovering *The Secret of the Swiss Chalet*, had been faced with many tense situations. Now a new mystery had presented itself.

"My mother's brother, Captain Tracy Forsythe," Kim began, "lives in Chincoteague. We haven't seen him for ten years. We're going to try persuading him to go back to England with us."

Captain Tracy Forsythe, Kim continued, was one of the dearest, handsomest men she had ever known. He was now fifty-five years old, and she wondered how much he might have changed in appearance since she had last seen him. At forty-five he had been tall and broad-shouldered, with thick blond hair and a ruddy complexion.

"He was not married, and usually stayed with us when he was ashore," Kim went on. "Uncle Tracy was master of a beautiful sailing ship called the *Sea Ghost*. Mr. Cooper, the owner, built it to resemble one in the story of *The Flying Dutchman*."

"Oh, you mean the phantom ship in the opera," said Louise, and Kim nodded.

She went on to say that Mr. and Mrs. Cooper and their son Claude, residents of London, often took long trips in the *Sea Ghost*. At this point in the story Kim's expression became very serious. She looked steadily at the stateroom floor before proceeding.

"One night in a dense fog in the Irish Sea," Kim resumed finally, "the *Sea Ghost* rammed a freighter. Several people on both ships lost their lives. Among them were Mr. and Mrs. Cooper."

"How dreadful!" said Louise.

"But Claude was saved?" Jean asked.

"Yes. He was fourteen then. The shock of his parents' death was terrible. He was also distressed because Uncle Tracy, whom he adored, was blamed for the accident."

"Was this proved?" Louise queried.

"It was proved to the satisfaction of the court," Kim replied, a note of bitterness in her voice. "But Dad and Mother and I have always felt that Uncle Tracy was not responsible for the accident. We think we now have proof of this."

Kim went on to say that her father had recently received a strange message from a hospital superintendent. A member of the crew of the ill-fated *Sea Ghost*, just before his death in the hospital, had dictated a memorandum. It said that on the night of the fatal accident, he had seen someone appear through the thick fog and strike Captain Forsythe so hard that he had fallen to the deck. Then the assailant had taken command and a few minutes later the collision had occurred.

"The crewman had not spoken up all these years because he had suspected Michael Fales, the harsh first mate, of the attack and feared his life would be in danger if he revealed this information."

"And your poor uncle never could prove his innocence?" Louise asked sympathetically.

Kim shook her head. "He was found unconscious, and afterward had no recollection about the accident. What was worse, Uncle Tracy's memory on happenings leading up to the crash was a blank."

The English girl told the Danas that the captain, in disgrace and out of a job, had decided to retire, take his savings, and come to America.

"He traveled around your country hunting for a little seashore village which would remind him of the fishing port where he had lived as a boy. That's why he settled in Chincoteague, where the original white settlers spoke Elizabethan English. The present inhabitants have kept many of the old expressions and Uncle Tracy feels at home there."

Kim went on, "My father looked up Michael Fales's record since the ship accident. I guess the crewman was right—Fales is a dangerous person. He has been in prison several times on robbery charges. Right now he is wanted in England for stealing a large sum of money, but apparently he has slipped out of our country. The police have not been able to find him."

"Do you think he too might have come to America?" Louise suggested.

Kim was thoughtful. "That is a possibility."

"What does Michael Fales look like?" Jean inquired.

Kim described him as a man of medium height with very dark, penetrating eyes. When last seen he had a heavy fringe of black beard.

"Would you know him on sight?" Louise asked.

"I doubt it," Kim replied. "I was only eleven years old the last time I was on the *Sea Ghost*, but Mother would recognize him."

Kim said that she must go now and pack her own bags. She would see the girls after dinner.

That evening at Captain Dana's table there was much merriment among the Danas and the other passengers, who enjoyed the festive farewell meal. Uncle Ned teased his nieces about trying to find pirate treasure, but wished them luck.

He winked at Aunt Harriet. "Bet a barnacle our girls'll dig up an adventure, anyhow."

When dinner was finished, the captain said to his family, "I'll have to say good-by to you at this time. From now until long after we dock I'll be busy. Enjoy your trip."

The next morning everyone was on deck early to watch for the Statue of Liberty, with the skyscrapers of Manhattan in the background.

Within two hours the *Balaska's* passengers had debarked and gone through customs. The Danas and their English friends said good-by.

"We'll ring you up as soon as we have plane

reservations for Salisbury," Kim called gaily to Louise, Jean, and Doris.

The others went sight-seeing but at five o'clock rode to the East Side Airlines Terminal and took a limousine to Newark Airport. There Aunt Harriet and the girls had dinner in an attractive restaurant. Afterward they went to the waiting room where they had arranged to meet the pilot of the chartered plane. Ted Mertz was a handsome ex-Navy flier, with thick, red hair and brilliant blue eyes.

He suggested that Miss Dana and Evelyn say good-by to the others at this time, since it was a long walk to his plane. Then Louise, Jean, Doris, and a porter followed the pilot. It was already dusk when they boarded the craft.

Ted Mertz introduced the girls to the copilot, steward, and ten other passengers, who were traveling in a group on official business for the National Advisory Space Administration base near Chincoteague.

"The airfield where we'll land is on the mainland, even though it's known as Chincoteague Airport," the pilot explained to the girls as they took took places and fastened their seat belts. "I think I'll be able to go as low as fifteen hundred feet and you will be able to see more of the coastline."

During the last fifteen minutes of the flight the girls went to talk to Ted and tell him how much they had enjoyed the trip. As they chatted, there suddenly came the sound of uneven firing from one of the plane's engines. The girls stared outside in alarm.

"What's wrong?" Louise asked worriedly.

The pilot's face was grave. He explained that one engine had gone out and he was unable to feather the other. "I'll have to contact the airport and give the distress signal." He quickly called into the radio, "May Day! May Day! May Day!"

After explaining to the man in the control tower that he was unable to gain enough altitude to reach Chincoteague airfield and would have to make an emergency landing nearby, Ted tried to reassure the girls. He said:

"We're almost directly over Assateague Island, next to Chincoteague. There's a sandy strip at the end called Fishing Point. Looks like a sea fog is rolling in, but I think I can come down there. You go back to your seats and strap yourselves in tight."

As Louise, Jean, and Doris re-entered the cabin, the pilot announced over the loud-speaker that he was making a forced landing. He instructed the passengers to fasten their seat belts securely, brace themselves for a big bump, and remain calm.

Doris and the Danas gripped the arms of their chairs and closed their eyes as the plane descended.

CHAPTER II

The Missing Captain

AFTER a few tense moments, the plane landed with a jar. Only their safety belts kept the girls from hitting the seats in front of them.

The craft bounced through the sand for a short distance. Then, turning sharply to the right, it stopped short. Jean was thrown against the window, banging her head, while Louise fell against her sister's shoulder. Doris, seated across the aisle from them, was also thrown sideways.

There was complete silence for a few seconds, then came groans from several of the passengers. A woman cried hysterically, "My arm is broken!"

The Danas quickly unfastened their seat belts. Finding themselves only bruised, the sisters got up to offer their assistance to others, including Doris, who was badly shaken up. They unstrapped her seat belt and helped her to her feet.

Louise, glancing up into the cockpit, saw that the pilot was slumped in his seat. The copilot lay sprawled on the floor. Louise rushed forward to see what she could do. She helped the copilot pick himself up, but he dropped into his seat, shaking his head in a dazed manner.

Louise turned to Ted Mertz. "You're hurt!" she said, seeing the look of pain on his face.

"Terribly sorry about all this," the pilot replied. "I'm afraid that I can't be of much help to anybody. I think I've shattered my knee."

Ted picked up his microphone and tried to contact the airport. "More bad luck," he said woefully. "The radio's dead."

"Is there any other way of getting help?" Louise asked.

The pilot nodded. "There's a National Park station about half a mile from here, but in this fog I'm afraid that a stranger never could find it."

"Jean and I can certainly try," Louise told him. "Which direction is it?"

"Due east of here." From a pocket Ted pulled a small compass and a flashlight. "If you use these, I guess you won't get lost. But be mighty careful. Ask one of the men to go with you."

Louise walked back and announced the plan to the other passengers. They were relieved to learn that assistance was within reach. However, none of the men aboard was able to make the journey with the girls. They had been injured too seriously to attempt the arduous hike through heavy damp sand and fog. The steward had twisted his ankle and could not walk.

"Let's go!" Jean urged her sister. "We can make it alone."

She and Louise grabbed jackets and left the plane. In the swirling fog the girls could see no more than five feet in front of them despite their flashlight. Then, suddenly, they noticed a beam of light sweeping in their direction.

"That must be the Assateague lighthouse," Louise surmised.

"I doubt that we'd ever find the National Park station without it," Jean said.

Two flashes close together came every forty seconds and during that period the girls made good time. In dark intervals they crept along with the aid of the small flashlight until the next big beam penetrated the fog.

Louise held the illuminated dial of the magnet compass in front of her and struck a course due east. But progress was slow, and even though the girls removed their shoes, they constantly turned their ankles in the uneven sandy soil. Several times they lost their balance completely and went down on their knees.

"I feel as if I've walked at least five miles," Jean complained. Nearly half an hour had gone by and they could still see no light but the beam from Assateague. They plodded on, however, hopeful that presently they would reach the Park Service station.

Suddenly Jean caught Louise's arm. "Listen!" she whispered intensely. "I thought I heard someone call."

The sisters stood still and listened. Jean had not been mistaken. From somewhere to their left came a man's voice. "Hello! Park Service searching! Hello! Park Service searching for plane!"

Overjoyed, both girls cried out, "Over here!"

"We hear you!" came an answering shout.

In a few seconds a powerful flashlight was turned in their direction and two young men appeared out of the fog. "We were looking for a plane we thought might have made a forced landing," one of them said, amazed at seeing two girls alone.

When the men had identified themselves as Green and Holman, temporary assistants at the station, Louise explained what had happened. She added that there were several passengers and crew members aboard the downed plane who needed medical aid.

"We'll send help at once," Green replied.

From his pocket he drew a two-way radio to the Park Service station. In a moment he was reporting the accident. The two men were instructed to go directly to the plane with the

"Listen!" Jean whispered. "I thought I heard
someone call!"

girls. Jeeps would bring medical supplies and stretchers.

Green turned to Louise and Jean. "Exactly where is the plane?"

"Due west from here," Louise answered. "We're not far from the end of the island."

Green relayed the girl's information to the station, then signed off. The trek back to the plane began. With the aid of the men's flashlights, the return trip was far less arduous. They reached the grounded craft just as two jeeps arrived.

When the Danas entered the plane, just ahead of the men, the passengers exclaimed in relief. Doris grabbed her friends' hands fervently. "You girls are simply marvelous!" she said. "I don't see how you did it."

Louise and Jean smiled, then turned to offer their help to the Park Service men who had immediately begun giving first aid to the injured. Since the only method of transportation was by jeep, the passengers and crew decided that the most seriously injured should be taken to the nearest Coast Guard station. The others could stay on board the plane overnight, in charge of the copilot and steward.

The latter asked Louise and Jean to serve hot tea and coffee and crackers from the emergency rations. By the time the snack had been eaten and the sisters had put away the cups, they were exhausted. They sank into their seats, tilted them to a comfortable position, and soon were asleep.

The Danas awoke to a clear, sunny day and looked out their window. They were not far from the ocean side of Fishing Point and to their delight they saw a Coast Guard boat waiting to transport them to Chincoteague. They awakened Doris and the three girls quickly went to wash and comb their hair. They were the last passengers to leave the plane.

"How's Ted Mertz?" Louise asked the chief petty officer of the rescue boat.

"A Navy copter came over and took him to the hospital," the man replied. "He'll be all right when they get his knee fixed up."

As the boat rounded the end of Fishing Point and headed across the blue water toward Chincoteague Island, the girls looked about eagerly. To their right lay a large cove with the Park Service station on the shore. Before them was Assateague Island, its high sand dunes thickly wooded with pine trees. The sturdy lighthouse, painted with wide red and white bands, stood at the peak.

Their boat bore left and entered a canal which led through a marshy area at the end of Chincoteague Island into Chincoteague Channel. All along the shore of the island were oystermen's homes and workshops. At several of the docks scowlike oyster boats were tied up.

Presently the town of Chincoteague came into

view, its many small white homes set back from the water. On the docks were the oysterhouses where the oysters were shucked, canned, and packed in ice for shipment all over the world.

"You'll find the people here very friendly," the chief petty officer told the girls. "They're plain—no society—and they're good, kindhearted folks. You will like them."

The rescue boat pulled into a dock near the bridge and causeway which led to the mainland. News of the plane's forced landing the night before had spread through the little town and a great crowd had gathered to welcome the last passengers to arrive. Mr. and Mrs. Harland rushed forward and hugged their daughter.

As they welcomed Louise and Jean warmly, Mrs. Harland declared, "If anything had happened to you girls, I never could have faced your aunt and uncle."

"I guess we were lucky," said Jean.

The girls' suitcases were set ashore and three young men standing nearby picked them up. One of them asked, "Are you aimin' to put up at the Channel Bass Hotel?"

"Yes, we are," Louise replied, smiling.

The group walked across the bridge to the main street of Chincoteague. The hotel was only a few short blocks away. It was an attractive, three-story structure with a glass-enclosed front porch.

They went into the cozy lobby and the girls registered. Then Mrs. Harland led them to the sofa across the room to meet local friends of theirs, Mr. and Mrs. Wolfe.

"We are so thankful you are safe," Mrs. Wolfe said kindly, and her husband added, "Our fogs can be quite terrifying."

Doris spoke up. "Mother, we're starved. Could we have some breakfast?"

"Yes, indeed. Suppose you girls go upstairs to your rooms and change to sport clothes. Dad and I will meet you in the dining room."

Twenty minutes later they sat down in the quaint room dotted with bright-red tablecloths. The girls ordered orange juice, bacon, scrambled eggs, and hot chocolate.

At a nearby table sat an elderly man, evidently a retired oysterman, drinking a bottle of soda, and a young couple eating large platefuls of fried oysters. The girls later learned that this was a midmorning snack for some of the townspeople who rose very early.

During the meal, Mr. Wolfe came to speak to the Danas and Harlands. He said he would be glad to tell them anything they wished to know about Chincoteague. Louise immediately asked him if he was acquainted with Captain Forsythe.

"Oh, I know him well," Mr. Wolfe replied. "He has lived near the hotel for ten years—that is, he did until six months ago."

Louise was startled. "You mean he has moved away?"

Mr. Wolfe explained that six months before, Captain Forsythe had told the owner of his apartment that he was going on a trip to accomplish a certain mission. The captain would not return until this had been done.

"What did he mean?" Jean asked, mystified.

Mr. Wolfe told them he did not know, nor did anyone else in Chincoteague. "Apparently the captain wanted to keep the purpose of his trip a secret."

The Danas, as well as Doris, knew that the Honeywells would be dreadfully disappointed.

Mr. Wolfe was called to the telephone and the girls began to speculate on the reason for the captain's trip. Doris told her parents in low tones who the Honeywells were, and how she and the Danas had learned about Captain Forsythe.

"Do you suppose the captain's mysterious trip has anything to do with the accident to the ship he used to sail?" Doris wondered. "Or perhaps he's hunting for the buried pirate treasure."

Louise and Jean were more inclined to think that the captain's disappearance did have something to do with the *Sea Ghost* tragedy. It was possible that he, as well as the Honeywells, had learned something about Michael Fales.

"Who knows?" Louise mused. "Mr. Fales may have escaped to the United States after stealing that money in England. He might be in this very area!" she added in a whisper.

When Mr. Wolfe returned to the table, Louise asked him if he had ever heard of a Michael Fales.

"I don't recognize the name," the man replied. "What does he look like?"

Louise described Fales, and mentioned the fact that he sometimes wore a heavy fringe of black beard.

Just then the elderly man at the nearby table called over, "I heard what you said, and I'm just a-wonderin' about somethin'. A feller that looks like that come into town a while back. He asked me a heap o' questions about Captain Forsythe."

The Dana girls and Doris were electrified by this information. Jean urged quickly, "Please tell us everything about him."

The man took a long swallow of soda before answering. Then he said, "The feller told me his name was Smith and that he come from London."

The speaker stood up and walked to the visitors' table. Leaning over, he added confidentially, "I never did believe him, somehow. And then one day I see a tattoo on his arm. In the middle of it was two initials. M.F."

CHAPTER III

A Bearded Suspect

"THOSE initials M.F. in the tattoo could stand for Michael Fales!" Jean exclaimed.

"Just what I was thinkin'," said the elderly man, and he took another swallow of his soda.

Louise asked him where the man, who used the name Smith, could be found. Their informant shrugged. "I haven't seen the feller around lately. If I do, I'll let you know. Well, I got to be gettin' along now," he added, and bade them good-by.

"Oh dear!" Doris looked fearful. "What if Michael Fales has gone after Captain Forsythe! He may harm him again!"

"I agree," said Louise, "but I can't understand why. It seems to me that if Fales is wanted by the police he would shave off his beard and disappear to a place where no one would recognize him."

"Yes," Jean agreed. "Some pretty strong incentive must have brought him here. I wonder what it could be."

"Maybe Captain Forsythe has something he wants," Louise stated.

She urged that the three girls query people in town to see if they could find out where Mr. Smith was.

As soon as they finished breakfast, the three excused themselves and set off. On the theory that Smith probably had rented a car or a boat, they inquired first at a garage. The Englishman had not been there.

Then the three chums separated to continue their sleuthing at the many boat landings to find out if Smith had hired a craft. Doris found a man who had rented Smith a speedboat about a week before. When she reported this to the Danas, they went back with her to question the owner further.

His answers were startling. "This Smith from London seemed to have plenty of money with him. He even offered to pay me for the boat in case he should wreck it, or not come back," the man went on. "And Smith pulled so much money from his pockets my eyes almost popped out o' my head."

"Was it English money?" Louise asked quickly.

"Why, yes, it was," the Chincoteaguean replied in surprise. "But I didn't have any trouble changin' it into good old American dollars.

"I didn't care about rentin' my speedboat to a stranger. But we went out together and he handled the boat as if he'd always lived around Chincoteague Bay. Smith didn't say, but I reckon he'd been right handy with a tiller and a wheel in his own country."

"Have you seen this man Smith since he took the boat?" Jean inquired.

"No. I reckoned it wasn't exactly fittin' to ask him where he was goin'."

The girls thanked the man for his information and hurried back to the hotel. They relayed their findings to Mr. and Mrs. Harland, and said that they would like to rent a boat and make a trip to Pirate Island.

"That's where Chris thinks the pirate treasure is buried," Jean explained. "And there's a chance that Captain Forsythe has gone there."

"And even Michael Fales," Doris put in.

Mr. Harland was due to leave for the mainland on business in a few minutes, but Mrs. Harland said she would accompany the girls on the trip if they could find a pilot and a boat. Louise consulted Mrs. Wolfe, who highly recommended Nat Steelman, former Oyster Inspector of the Chincoteague area.

"If he's not busy, I know he'll be glad to take you. He has a fast little cruiser."

"Thank you," said Louise. "Where can we find him?"

"I'll phone his house. If he isn't there and he's not out on the bay, he'll be down at a dock just the other side of the bridge."

While Mrs. Wolfe was telephoning, Mrs. Harland gave a word of caution to the young sleuths. "I think it would be best for you to keep your suspicions about this man Smith to yourselves. You know how news spreads in a small place. If he's really Michael Fales and is trying to hide, he would certainly be alerted."

The girls nodded as Mrs. Wolfe came back from the telephone and reported that Nat Steelman was at the dock. The Danas and Harlands went to their rooms for sweaters, then set off to find the former oyster inspector.

Nat Steelman had a rugged physique and kind eyes. He greeted them with a friendly smile and said he would be happy to make the trip to Pirate Island.

"Do you aim to find the buried treasure?" he teased the girls as he cast off.

Louise countered with a question. "Do you think it's still there?"

"I never heard tell of anyone digging it up," Nat Steelman replied, his eyes twinkling.

He stepped into the small cabin of his boat and started the engine. Mrs. Harland and the girls seated themselves in canvas-backed chairs on the afterdeck of the cruiser.

Presently their pilot called out, "We'll keep fairly close to the coast of Assateague on our way to Pirate Island. Then you may see some of the wild ponies grazing along the shore."

He took the same route which the Coast Guard

rescue boat had used, but upon reaching Tom's Cove at the end of the canal, he turned north. After they had gone about five nautical miles, he pointed out an oyster boat with men dredging and bringing up quantities of the famous Chincoteague mollusks.

"The baby oysters are planted in various spots," Nat Steelman explained, "and then are harvested two to three years later."

"And what is that long, narrow float?" Doris asked him.

"You've named it right," Nat Steelman replied. "Sometimes the men dig up more oysters than they can carry away. This usually happens when there's very low tide and the men with the boats can't get to the spots. Those floats are built so the center part can be lowered with block and tackle. Oysters are heaped up on them and the centers are let down into the water. You know, an oyster has to be kept cold or it will spoil. This float system isn't used much any more."

As he spoke, the cruiser sped past the wooded hillside of Assateague.

"You wouldn't want a prettier sight," Nat Steelman said proudly. "When I was just a little fellow I used to go over to Assateague a lot. My great-grandmother lived there. She was part Indian, like most everybody else around here. She'd learned a lot of secrets from the Indians about using herbs—they grow wild over there."

"Have the secrets come down through your family?" Mrs. Harland spoke up.

"Unfortunately no," Nat Steelman answered. "I was always going to find out about my great-grandmother's concoctions. But first thing I knew she was gone and the secrets died with her."

"That's too bad," said Doris.

"Yes, 'tis," Nat Steelman agreed, "because the dear old lady sure could cure people. I heard many times how folks that the doctors had given up for near death had come to her and been cured by herbs. She used to say the secret was to purify the blood."

The cruiser passed the lighthouse, then Piney Island, then Morris Island, finally passing Wildcat Point and coming out into Chincoteague Bay.

As Doris looked toward the shore of Assateague, she remarked, "This certainly is a deserted place. A good spot to get lost in!"

Nat Steelman laughed. "You're right, miss. I've often thought if I was trying to run away and hide from people, I'd go in past Ragged Point or maybe a little farther along where we come to the Toby Islands. On Assateague, opposite them, there are all sorts of little hidden waterways."

The girls had not missed one word of the man's last statement. They speculated that maybe Michael Fales planned to hide in one of these places, wait for an opportunity to harm Captain Forsythe, and steal something valuable from him!

Louise whispered to Mrs. Harland that she felt sure the former inspector could be trusted with their secret. Doris' mother nodded and Louise walked forward to the cabin.

"Did you happen to meet a Mr. Smith of London who was visiting Chincoteague?" she asked.

"No, I can't say I did, but I've heard of the man. Do you know him?"

Louise said no, then told him of the girls' suspicion that the name Smith was an alias. "We thought Mr. Smith might be hiding somewhere around here, trying to find the treasure, or more probably, doing some stealing."

Nat Steelman gave Louise a long searching look. "Are you meaning that this Mr. Smith may be running away from the law?"

"I'm afraid so," Louise replied. Then she told him the whole story and said they might possibly identify Fales by his fringe of beard and the initialed tattoo on his arm.

"That's a right worrisome situation," Nat Steelman remarked. "I'll sure keep my eyes open for him. We don't want folks like that around here."

They had covered almost another seven miles when the girls spotted a man in a speedboat near a group of small islands.

"What is that place ahead?" Jean asked their pilot.

"It's where we're going. The whole group is

called Pirate Island. It's said that there was only one island at the time the treasure was buried."

Louise asked for the pilot's binoculars and trained them on the speedboat ahead. The man had his back to her and she could not tell whether or not he was bearded. Suddenly he seemed to become aware of the oncoming boat, and turned. Louise gasped. He wore a fringe of black beard! The next instant he started his motor and hurried away.

"That must be Michael Fales!" Louise cried out. "Let's chase him!"

With a spurt of speed the cruiser cleaved through the water and soon overtook the suspect.

"Stop!" Nat Steelman called out.

The bearded man cut his motor and glared at his pursuers. "What do you want of me?"

"Is your name Smith and are you from London?" Jean called out.

"No."

Louise had been looking at the man's arms. His shirt sleeves were rolled up high. There was no tattoo on either arm. "We're sorry to have bothered you, but we're looking for a bearded man," she explained. "We thought surely you must be the one, so that's why we chased your boat."

"I don't have to talk to people if I don't want to," the stranger said defiantly.

Louise smiled at him. "Of course you don't, but

will you please answer one question? Do you know, or have you ever heard of a man around here named Michael Fales?"

"Yes, I do, and that's the reason I ran away from you. Michael's a cousin of mine and no good. People keep coming after me all the time asking me where he is and trying to get money out of me to pay his bills. That's why I came out here, thinking I'd get a little peace and quiet. And now you come along with the same question."

His listeners were astounded. It had been evident from early in the conversation that this man was not English, although his cousin was.

"Did you know your cousin is wanted by the police in England?" Doris questioned.

"Well, that's a good one." The man in the speedboat looked puzzled. "It couldn't possibly be true. My cousin Mike's never been out of the United States. For me, I wish he'd go to the North Pole and get lost. Say," the man added suddenly, "I reckon you folks and I aren't talking about the same man."

"It certainly sounds that way," Louise agreed. "Your cousin is not English?"

"No, certainly not. And what did you call him?"

"Michael Fales."

At this the stranger began to laugh. "Well, we're all mixed up. My cousin's name isn't Fales, it's Sayles. So I guess now we're all squared away."

The Danas and their friends apologized for the

mistake. The man laughed, saying, "It's okay." Nat Steelman put on power and they started for the little group of islands that formed Pirate Island. As the cruiser circled the area the girls were surprised to find the islands treeless and covered only by marsh grass. No one was in sight, but Louise and Jean were eager to wade ashore to try their luck at finding a clue that might lead to Captain Forsythe.

"I'll go with you," Doris spoke up.

The girls took off their sneakers, tucked them under their arms, and splashed through the water onto the shore. A concentrated search of the central island in the group went on for several minutes.

Then, suddenly, Doris called out excitedly, "Girls! Come over here quick! I've found a clue!"

CHAPTER IV

A Shoreline Search

"WHAT do you think of this?" Doris asked, as she opened her hand and showed Louise and Jean a coin. "It's English."

As Louise took the coin and examined it, she remarked, "Your guess is that Captain Forsythe or Michael Fales dropped it?"

"That's right. Look at the date on the coin. It's a modern one, so it couldn't have belonged to an old pirate."

The Danas admitted that both Doris' find and her deduction were very good. "Maybe one or the other of those men is still around here," Jean observed.

"If he is, he must have a boat hidden some place," Louise decided.

The girls returned to the cruiser and asked Nat Steelman to go as close as he could to the shores of Assateague, hoping they might spot a boat secreted in some little cove or lagoon. But their search was fruitless.

Presently they came to a place where a slight depression in the hillside was noticeable. "See that?" the former inspector asked. "Once an inlet ran through there from the ocean to the bay. That's the route they say the pirate Charles Wilson took when he buried his treasure."

Nat Steelman told his passengers that the tides in the bay built the constantly shifting sands into shoals, and eventually into islands. "Lots of these islands that you're seeing now weren't even here when I was a little boy!"

"Nature is strange and wonderful," Mrs. Harland remarked.

Steelman nodded. "You're right, ma'am. She can be a lot deceiving, and yet she can build the prettiest things you want to look at. You can't tell nothing about her."

"I suppose," Doris put in, "that seeds are brought to the islands by the sea and wind, and that's the way the woods are planted. What grows in them?"

The pilot said that most of the trees were known as bull pine. "Then there are lots of huckleberries, blackberries, wild honeysuckle, and thornbushes. If you go ashore sometime, be careful of the thornbushes and the prickly thorn trees. Some of the thorns in those bushes are sharp as needles and ten inches long!"

"I'll remember." Doris nodded her head emphatically.

There was no conversation for a while as the group watched the shoreline further for any sign of a moored boat.

Presently Jean asked, "Mr. Steelman, were the wild ponies brought to Assateague?"

"Well, not exactly. The first horses to come here swam ashore from a wrecked Spanish galleon early in the sixteenth century. It's said that actually they came to Chincoteague, which had trees and grass, instead of Assateague which was not much more than a long shoal. But later, when the shoal became a wooded island, the ponies were driven to Assateague by the inhabitants of Chincoteague.

"The original ancestors of today's wild ponies were fine Arabian horses being shipped to Peru from Spain." Nat Steelman smiled. "But nobody would recognize their descendants today. They're not sleek, but have heavy, shaggy coats. They're much smaller in size and their fur is of various combinations of black, brown, and white. Say, look over there! Some ponies are coming down toward the water now."

The Danas were eager to get a closer look at the ponies. The pilot obligingly turned his craft and went as near the shoreline as he dared. A stallion and several brood mares had started to pull up mouthfuls of the salt grass.

Upon hearing the sound of the cruiser's engine, they all looked up and stared at the visitors. Apparently satisfied that the boat's passengers were harmless, the ponies calmly turned their backs to the audience and began to feed again.

The girls laughed and Louise remarked, "They don't seem very wild."

"But you should see them on Pony Penning Day," the former inspector remarked.

"What happens then?" Jean asked.

"Well, first of all," Nat Steelman explained, "the watermen of Chincoteague turn cowboys for a few days. They take their horses over to Assateague on boats, then they have a real roundup. A stallion always stays with his brood mares, so that makes it easy to find bands of ponies. One by one they're driven to a certain point. It's the narrowest part of the channel—about one-eighth of a mile wide.

"They are made to swim over to Chincoteague and are driven to the auction spot. People come from all around to buy the ponies. Some are taken away, others are left here to be broken to the saddle and sold the next year. The ones that nobody buys are sent back to Assateague."

"And I'll bet they're glad to get there!" Jean said, grinning.

After hearing the story, Doris was quiet for some time. Louise noticed that her friend was frowning and asked why.

Doris said she was worried. "Suppose Captain Forsythe was staying all alone on Assateague and some of the wild ponies trampled him!"

Louise and Jean turned toward Nat Steelman and asked what he thought of this possibility. The pilot pondered the idea for a moment. "I suppose anything could happen, but my impression of Captain Forsythe is that he knew how to take care of himself. Besides, he's lived around here long enough to learn the ways of the wild ponies."

"Have you any idea where Captain Forsythe went?" Jean asked the pilot.

"No, but maybe on a long trip. He went off in the speedboat he owns. I heard that from a waterman several months ago."

Nat Steelman now throttled his motor and reached into a locker. From it he brought out cans of frankfurters, tins of crackers, and bottles of soda. "I reckon you folks must be right hungry," he remarked. He opened the cans of food and handed them to Louise to pass. Then he snapped off the caps on the bottles and gave a bottle to each of his passengers.

"How did you know I was starving?" Jean asked, grinning at the pilot.

After finishing the tasty lunch, Nat Steelman gave his boat power. The return trip along the shores of Assateague was made without the Danas and the Harlands sighting any abandoned or hidden boat.

After they reached Chincoteague dock, and Mrs. Harland had paid their guide, Louise asked him if he would be able to take them on further trips.

Nat Steelman smiled. "I'll be right tied up for the next few days. But if you want to do some more detective work, I know just the man for you. He spends a lot of time on Chincoteague—likes to fish and hunt. He has a nice little cruiser and a right smart dinghy with an outboard motor that he trails behind. He can take that dinghy into the shallowest water. I believe it would be exactly what you might need to do your searching."

Nat Steelman said the man's name was Sam Everett. "If you look him up, just say I sent you."

Mrs. Harland and the girls thanked the former inspector for the trip and for suggesting another pilot. Then they hurried off across the bridge and up the street to the hotel. The lobby was quiet except for the sound of a man singing to the accompaniment of a banjo. The words were very sad, and the singer was including the proper sobbing tremolos for effect.

Despite the sorrowful nature of the ballad, the girls had to smile at the singer's great fervor. "Let's go see him," Jean suggested.

The girls walked into the comfortable dining room. An elderly man, wearing a soft felt hat pushed part way back on his head, sat strumming a banjo as he sang with feeling.

"She's never comin' back no more, no more,
My Annie's never comin' back no more
She's a-sittin' with the angels, pretty, pretty an-
gels.
My Annie's never comin' back no more, no
more."

The three girls walked quietly down the aisle between the tables until they reached the singer. Before they had a chance to speak to him, a young man hurried from a back room and came up to the group. He greeted the girls, then turned and added:

"Pop, don't you know there are ladies present? It's fittin' for you to take off your hat."

Pop looked up from his banjo and grinned. "Why don't you know, son, I couldn't play a note nor sing a word without my hat on!"

CHAPTER V

An Annoying Delay

POP *could not play nor sing with his hat off!*

Though Louise, Jean, and Doris thought this very amusing, they respected the elderly man's feelings and smiled at him encouragingly.

He needed no more invitation than this to render another ballad. This one was in a humorous vein—about a sailor who rode around the ocean on a mythological sea horse taking booty from unwary islanders.

When Pop finished singing, the girls grinned and clapped. Then Jean asked, "Is that a local song? I've never heard it before."

Pop shook his head. "No. I just learned it lately. Guess it's probably English. But I know all the local songs too. Ought to. Lived up and down these coasts all my life."

"You mean Chincoteague, Assateague, and the mainland too?" Doris inquired.

Pop quickly informed her that nobody lived on

Assateague any more. "Used to be a village near the lighthouse. Nice place too. But after they put in the causeway from Chincoteague to the mainland, all the folks moved out of the village and come over here."

Louise had been staring into space during the past few seconds as an idea formulated in her mind. She asked Pop where he had learned the English ballad he had sung.

"Well, I can answer that question easy. There was an English feller come here a couple of weeks ago. Name of Smith. Heard me singin' and asked where I lived. I told him and he come to my place a couple of times. Said he liked to sing sea chanteys but hadn't had a chance since he was a young'un. We had a right good time together. That's when he taught me the one 'bout the man on the sea horse."

The three girls were intensely interested in this new bit of information. Was he the Mr. Smith they wanted to find? Louise asked Pop several questions concerning the man.

The banjoist could answer only a few of them, but he did say that he had the impression Smith had run away from England because he had gotten into some kind of trouble.

"What kind?" Louise queried, sure now he was Michael Fales.

"That I can't rightly say," Pop replied. He chuckled. "Maybe his wife nagged him too much. You know, boys and men often light out and sign up on ships just to get away from troubles at home."

The girls made no comment. They were gathering more and more evidence that Mr. Smith of London was indeed the Michael Fales who had run away from England.

Recalling what they had learned from the man who rented the speedboat to Smith, they felt sure that the English money he had used to pay for it was part of the funds he had stolen in his own country. It was even possible that he was carrying all the rest of the loot around with him!

"Do you know where this Mr. Smith is now?" Louise asked Pop.

The elderly man shook his head. "Haven't seen him about in over a week," he replied.

During the last part of the conversation the girls had been aware of the telephone ringing in the lobby. Now Louise was summoned to take the call. As she said hello, a girl's voice on the other end of the line asked, "Are you there, Louise? This is Kim."

"Kim! It's wonderful to hear from you. Oh, we have so much to tell you and your mother. When are you coming down?"

Kim replied that they were leaving on a plane for Salisbury the following morning. "We'll arrive about ten. If you can meet us, it'll be jolly. If not, Mother and I will find other transportation to Chincoteague."

"We'll meet you if we possibly can," Louise promised. "Mr. Harland has to use his car, but I'm sure we can rent another. Give us until ten-thirty, then leave."

"Very good," Kim replied. "In any case, Mother and I will see you some time tomorrow. I can hardly wait to hear all you have to tell us."

When Doris heard the news, she hurried upstairs to inform her mother, then the Harlands and Danas set off to rent a car for the next morning. This did not prove to be as easy a task as they had thought. Finally they were directed to a garage where a new sedan was having its first checkup.

Mrs. Harland introduced herself to the garage owner and said, "We need a car for tomorrow and were told that we might be able to rent yours. Would this be possible? We want to drive to Salisbury airport and pick up some friends. We'll come directly back."

"I reckon that will be all right," the man replied. "I know you will take good care of her." He tapped the hood of the automobile. "Now when do you figure you want to take her?"

"Tomorrow morning about eight-thirty."

"Okay. She'll be down here waitin' for you. And I'll have her in front of the pump filled with gas. Just take her. Hope you have a safe journey," he added, smiling.

"Thank you very much," said Mrs. Harland. She and the owner discussed price for a few moments and as soon as this was settled, she and the girls went back to the hotel.

The following morning the travelers arrived promptly at the garage. The car they were renting stood ready at the side of the building. Mrs. Harland checked the gasoline gauge. The tank was three-quarters full.

Doris opened the car door for her mother, then climbed in beside her. The Danas settled themselves in the rear seat. In a few minutes they had crossed the bridge and were rolling along the causeway.

As they reached a marsh with a sign reading *Mosquito Creek,* Jean laughed. "I'd hate to pitch a tent around here if it's anything like its name!"

They rode on until they came to the main road, then turned right. They had gone no more than five miles when suddenly Mrs. Harland exclaimed, "Why, the gas tank is almost empty! I guess the gauge doesn't register correctly."

She pulled into the nearest service station and had the tank filled. The group started off once more, but had gone scarcely another five miles, when the indicator again showed the tank to be almost empty.

"I can't understand this," said Mrs. Harland worriedly. The girls too were perplexed.

Doris' mother drove into the first service station they came to. This time she asked the attendant to measure the gas in the tank to see if the indicator was working properly. The man reported that there was very little gas left in the tank. When Mrs. Harland told him what had happened earlier, he frowned.

"Sounds to me, ma'am, as if you got a hole in the tank," he explained.

"What!" Jean called out in amazement. "Why, this is a new car!"

"I can see it is," the attendant replied. "I'll take a look at the tank."

The mechanic asked Mrs. Harland to drive onto a hydraulic lift at one side of the service station. Then he raised the car up and walked underneath it to have a look.

"There's a hole in here all right," he said. "And it wasn't caused by rust. It looks as if somebody had punched it in deliberately."

Mrs. Harland and the girls were startled. Had some spiteful person done this as an unfriendly act against the car's owner? Or did they themselves have some enemy who was trying to keep them from getting to Salisbury in time to meet the Honeywells?

"Can you plug up the hole right away?" Mrs. Harland asked.

"Yes," the garageman answered. "I'll get a screw plug and patch the tank in right smart time."

Louise decided that while they were waiting she would phone the airport. She could have Mrs. Honeywell paged and given the message that the

Danas and Harlands would be a few minutes late. When Louise completed the call she returned to the group.

The garageman kept his word and within fifteen minutes the tank had been repaired and filled once more. The travelers were on their way. Mrs. Harland drove at the speed limit in order to get to the airport as quickly as possible, so that the Honeywells would not be kept waiting too long.

They arrived at ten forty-five, and while Mrs. Harland waited in the car, the three girls dashed into the waiting room to find their English friends.

"There they are!" Louise exclaimed, and hurried toward the Honeywells.

"Hello!" Jean called over her sister's shoulder. "Hope you haven't been waiting long."

"We're so glad you're here," said Kim. "I've been bursting to hear what you had to tell Mother and me."

Mrs. Honeywell suggested that first they put their bags into the car and start for Chincoteague. Kim added, "Fine. I'm frightfully eager to get to the island."

A porter wheeled the Honeywells' luggage out to the car. Mrs. Harland was introduced, and invited Kim's mother to sit up front with her. The four girls squeezed into the rear seat.

When the car started off, Kim begged the other girls to bring her up to date on all the news. As the automobile neared the entrance to the airport, Louise said, "I'll start at the beginning. First, we had to make a crash landing in dense fog off of Chincoteague."

"Oh, how dreadful!" Kim exclaimed. "Weren't you terribly—"

She did not finish the sentence, for at that moment those in the car became aware of a motorcycle policeman pulling up alongside and ordering Mrs. Harland to stop. She obeyed at once.

"I didn't realize I was breaking any law," she told the officer.

He smiled. "You weren't, madam," the officer assured her. "I came to tell you that the telephone operator in the air terminal is holding an important overseas call for Mrs. Honeywell."

"Oh dear, what can it be?" the English woman cried out in distress.

CHAPTER VI

Fire!

QUICKLY Mrs. Harland drove back to the entrance of the airport building. Mrs. Honeywell and Kim alighted and rushed inside. Doris' mother parked the car, then she and the girls went in also. They sat down and waited anxiously for the overseas telephone conversation to be concluded.

"Oh, I do hope Kim and her mother aren't receiving bad news!" Doris spoke up.

Mrs. Harland and the Danas nodded. There was little talk among the four, who watched the clock constantly. At last they saw Kim coming toward them, a grave expression on her face.

Louise jumped up to meet her. "Is something wrong at home, Kim?" she asked kindly.

"Not at home," the English girl replied. "But Dad received shocking news about Uncle Tracy. He's dead!"

"Oh!" Louise cried out. "How dreadful!"

When they reached the rest of the group, Kim

explained that the announcement of Captain For-sythe's passing actually had come to Claude Cooper. "You recall, he's the son of the man who owned the *Sea Ghost*."

As the other girls nodded, Kim told them that the news had reached him in a cable from a Salisbury lawyer named Samuel Tenney.

"Does he have charge of Captain Forsythe's estate?" Mrs. Harland asked.

"I don't know," Kim answered. "All my father said was that Claude is heartbroken. He had always hoped to see the captain again."

"Will this news change your plans?" Doris queried.

"I'm afraid so," Kim returned sadly. "My father was calling to say that there is no necessity now of our going to Chincoteague."

While the Danas and their friends attempted to comfort the Honeywells, Jean quietly excused herself and went to consult a telephone directory. She had decided to obtain Samuel Tenney's address, and then suggest that the Honeywells call on him for further details. To her amazement no Samuel Tenney was listed. Thinking the lawyer might have an unlisted number, she dialed the head operator and asked for this information.

After a few seconds' wait, the operator reported, "We have no Samuel Tenney, a lawyer, with an unlisted number."

Jean was surprised, but thought, "Maybe he's a

member of some law firm." She consulted a class-
ified telephone directory, which listed the names
of the law firms. One by one she called them. None
had ever heard of a Samuel Tenney.

Leaving the telephone booth, Jean said excitedly, "I believe that cable to Claude Cooper was a
fake!"

"Oh, I hope you're right!" Kim exclaimed. "If
so, Uncle Tracy is still living!"

"I hate to mention this," Doris spoke up, "but
it's possible Mr. Samuel Tenney doesn't live in
Salisbury and just happened to send the telegram
from here."

Jean offered to continue her sleuthing along
these lines. She decided to call the office of the
Maryland Bar Association. An information clerk
there seemed to prove Jean's contention about the
cable being a hoax—there was no Samuel Tenney
listed on their roster.

"What do you suggest we do now?" Kim asked
her friends.

Louise suggested that they go to the main telegraph office in town and if possible get a description of the person who had sent the cable. The
others agreed and they all hurried to the car. In a
short time they reached the office. Smiling, Louise
asked the clerk for the information.

"Oh, I remember the man who sent it," the clerk
replied promptly. "He spoke with an English accent."

"Was he supposed to be Samuel Tenney?" Louise inquired.

"I think so," the young man answered. "When I asked him to fill in the sender's address, he just said we could find him in the phone book and walked out."

"And you didn't know the man?" Louise prodded.

"Never saw him before in my life."

The clerk told Louise that the man had a heavy fringe of black beard. This, together with the English accent, convinced the Danas and their friends that it was Michael Fales, alias Mr. Smith of London, who had sent the cable!

"Did this man have a tattoo on one arm?" Louise asked.

The clerk grinned. "You sound like a detective. I don't know whether the man had a tattoo on his arm or not. He had on a long-sleeved sports jacket, so I couldn't see his bare arms."

Louise thanked the clerk for his help. Then the Danas and their friends left the telegraph office.

Louise and Jean, walking a short distance ahead of the others, began to talk over this latest development. Jean said fearfully, "Oh, that horrible Michael Fales may be trying to make the message in the cable come true!"

"Jean, you shouldn't think such dreadful things," Louise chided her sister. "I'm beginning to suspect, though, that he sent the cable as a hoax to keep the Honeywells away from Chincoteague. Fales just doesn't want them to find Captain Forsythe before he can carry out his own plans."

Doris and Kim caught up to the sisters and wanted to know what they were talking about. Louise repeated the Danas' theory.

Kim was shocked but made no comment until they reached the car. She told her mother the whole story, including the idea that Fales had come to America to steal something from Captain Forsythe.

"Mother, do you know of anything Fales might want?" she asked.

Mrs. Honeywell surprised the girls by revealing that her brother always carried with him a valuable pearl he had brought from the Orient. "But it wasn't found after the accident and it was assumed the pearl went down with the ship."

"But Fales probably thinks the captain has it," Louise surmised. "When Fales had to disappear, he decided to make profitable use of his time while in hiding."

"Oh, everything is so complicated," Kim said with a sigh. Then she burst out, "I'm going into the first telephone booth I see and put in an overseas call to Claude. He ought to know all that Louise and Jean have found out. Poor chap! If there's a possibility that Uncle Tracy is alive, Claude should know it immediately."

It was decided that they would go back to the

airport to make the call, since it probably would take some time to complete.

An hour later when Kim came from the telephone booth, she was smiling happily. "The most terrific thing has happened!" she exclaimed. "Claude is going to fly over here and meet us at Chincoteague. He says he wants to get at the truth of this matter himself!"

"I think that's a very good idea," her mother spoke up. "And, Kim darling, I have been mulling things over. We shall go on to Chincoteague at any rate."

"I'm glad you decided that," said Jean.

"I have another reason for going," said Mrs. Honeywell. "Friends of my brother's, the Kings, moved from England to a farm here in Maryland. The farm seems to be on our route. I suggest that we stop and call on the Kings. They may be able to provide a very good clue about Tracy."

The Danas were excited by this proposal. It might be a big help in solving the mystery!

The journey to Chincoteague was started once more. After they had driven a few miles, Mrs. Honeywell took the address of the Kings from her purse. "I believe their farm is about a mile beyond the next little town we come to," she remarked.

As they neared the spot, Mrs. Harland slowed down and they all began looking for the name *King* on a mailbox.

Suddenly Doris cried out, "That farmhouse just ahead! Smoke's pouring from the second-floor windows!"

Mrs. Harland put on speed and raced into the driveway past a mailbox marked *E. J. Dolan*. When they reached the two-story frame house they could see no sign of flames.

Just as they were wondering if anyone was at home, they saw a little girl lean far out of an upstairs window and scream, "Mommy! Daddy! I can't get out! The hall is full of smoke!"

By this time the girls and the two women had jumped out of the car. Doris rushed to the front door of the house and pounded on it. No response.

"It's too late to go inside and save that child," said Louise, her mind working rapidly. "We'll have to figure out a way to do it from here!"

On a nearby clothesline, among some articles hung out to dry, was a large-sized bed sheet. Dashing to the line, Louise unpinned the sheet and hurried back to the other girls.

Quickly realizing what Louise had in mind, the others grabbed the sides of the sheet and held it taut under the window.

"Jump!" Louise called up to the little girl. "We'll catch you in the sheet!"

"I'm afraid," the child cried in a panic-stricken voice.

Smoke was already swirling around her, but a

second later came a billowing wave of it. The little girl began to cough and choke.

"You must jump!" Louise insisted.

The child hesitated no longer. Climbing onto the window sill, she leaped forward and dropped neatly into the sheet.

"Thank goodness you're safe!" Mrs. Harland exclaimed. "Where are your mother and father?"

As the little girl, half sobbing, was lifted from the sheet, she pointed toward a field. "There they are!"

In the distance the farmer and his wife could be seen running across the furrowed field. "Debbie! Debbie!" they both called out. "Are you hurt?"

The visitors did not wait for the couple to reach the house. Seeing some buckets and milk cans near the side door, Mrs. Harland, Mrs. Honeywell, and Kim grabbed them and rushed to a well in the yard.

Louise, meanwhile, had spotted a garden hose and rushed over to unreel it. The hose ran from the inside of a small building, presumably a milk-house, and she hoped it was attached to the water system. As she turned the nozzle, water squirted out in a strong stream.

"I'll try to find out just where the fire is," Jean called out, dashing into the house.

A few seconds later she ran outdoors again. "Bring the hose in here!" she called. "The fire's in the second-floor hall!"

Louise turned off the water and raced into the

"Jump!" Louise called. "We'll catch you in
the sheet."

lower hall. Running halfway up the stairs, she opened the nozzle once more and squirted water into the swirling smoke above her.

Jean, meanwhile, had located a back stairway. As the rest of the group ran into the house with buckets and cans of water, she directed them to the rear set of steps.

By the time Jean returned to the front hall to see if she could help Louise, the farmer had arrived.

"Thank you so much for saving our child," he cried out. "We left her alone only a little while. She was taking her nap."

By this time the smoke had nearly cleared from the soaking-wet second-floor hallway.

"You—you all have put out the fire!" he said to Louise and Jean, as if he could hardly believe it.

"There was actually more smoke than fire," Jean reassured him. "I think it started in the hall closet." She pointed to a burned door. "That's the only place I saw any flames."

"My wife keeps some cleaning fluid and old rags in there," the farmer explained. "I guess that's what started the trouble." He looked at the damage ruefully. "I reckon the whole thing was my fault. I brought Debbie up here for her nap. I was smoking a cigarette and I did go into that closet for a rag. A spark must have dropped and ignited the cloth. Oh, how can we ever thank you for what you've done!"

Louise said smilingly that this was not necessary.

"I'm just glad we got here in time to help," she said. "And now I think we'd better hurry along. We're looking for people named King. Do you know where they live?"

"Just down the road a piece," the farmer replied.

When they reached the foot of the steps, Debbie's mother rushed up to the Danas and threw her arms around them. "Oh, you wonderful, wonderful girls!" she said, weeping.

A few minutes later Jean and Louise joined the rest of their group outside and climbed into the car. Debbie and her parents waved until the car was out of sight.

It was only a five-minute ride to the Kings' homestead. It was a neatly kept place, with bright-colored flowers of many varieties growing in profusion around it. As Mrs. Harland stopped in front of the house, the kitchen door opened and a man stepped outside.

"Mr. King?" Mrs. Honeywell asked, leaning from the car window.

"Yes, ma'am," he replied. "You wish to see me?"

Mrs. Honeywell, after introducing Kim, the Danas, and the Harlands, explained that she and her daughter were from London. The Kings' name had been given to them because the farmer was acquainted with her brother, Captain Forsythe, whom the Honeywells were hoping to find.

Mr. King frowned. "Are you inferring that Captain Forsythe has disappeared?"

"You didn't know it?" Mrs. Honeywell countered.

The man shook his head and said, "We haven't seen the captain for over six months. But when he was here last time he didn't say anything about going away."

"Have you any reason to believe that my brother may no longer be living?" Kim's mother asked hesitantly.

"Why, no. He was hale and hearty. And as for any trouble out on the water, it's not likely. Captain Forsythe was one of the finest English skippers you'd want to find."

Louise and Jean had stepped from the car and Louise asked, "Mr. King, can you give us any clue as to where Captain Forsythe might have gone?"

The farmer rubbed his chin thoughtfully with one hand and gazed across the field. He did not answer Louise for several seconds, then said, "This might sound a bit daft to you, but I think maybe the captain went to consult some kind of memory doctor."

"A memory doctor?" Louise repeated. "Do you mean a psychiatrist?"

"I guess you might call him that," Mr. King answered. "The captain seemed very moody the last time he came here. He wanted to do something to restore his memory about what happened the night of the accident to the *Sea Ghost*. You know about that, don't you?"

Louise nodded, then said reflectively to the Honeywells, "If Captain Forsythe has gone any distance to consult a psychiatrist, we may have a difficult time finding him."

"And it may take the searchers far from Chincoteague," Jean thought.

CHAPTER VII

Pirate Island Picnic

JEAN DANA did not mention her thought to anyone that Captain Forsythe might be far away from Chincoteague. But if so, it would mean that she and Louise would have to give up trying to solve the mystery.

"We're guests of Doris' parents," she told herself, as Mrs. Harland drove away from the King farmhouse, "and besides, the boys are coming down. Louise and I can't run off!"

Mrs. Harland drove a few miles farther, then pulled into the attractive dooryard of a small restaurant. "You must be ready to eat," she said, chuckling. "I had breakfast so long ago, it seems like yesterday!"

The others confessed to being very hungry and read the menu eagerly. Kim and her mother said they had never eaten fried oysters and would like to try them.

A little while later, as she dipped a crisp oyster into some tartar sauce, Mrs. Honeywell said, "Perfectly delicious!"

During the meal she and her friends continued to discuss the mystery concerning Captain Forsythe.

Louise had a theory. "We know he went off in his boat," she said. "If he were going to some doctor or psychiatrist, he probably went to one of the larger ports in Virginia or Maryland. As soon as we get to Chincoteague, let's find out the name and model of his speedboat. Then we can phone to the various ports to learn if he has been seen."

"I think that's a splendid idea," Mrs. Honeywell said. She smiled. "You girls amaze me with your detective instincts. I wish I had some of them. I'm afraid that without you I never would find my brother."

Louise and Jean laughed modestly, and Jean said, "Mrs. Honeywell, perhaps you'd better not pay us so many compliments until we solve the case!"

When the Danas and their friends reached the bridge leading into Chincoteague, Louise and Jean asked to be dropped off at the waterfront. "Maybe somebody around here can tell us about the captain's boat," Jean stated. "We'll meet you all at the hotel in a little while."

There were many watermen at the docks and the sisters soon learned the name and model of the speedboat which Captain Forsythe owned. The two girls walked quickly to the hotel, determined to make inquiries as to where the captain might have moored his boat. They consulted a detailed map, then a telephone directory. But none of their calls yielded any clue to the whereabouts of the craft.

"Before I give up," said Louise, "I'm going to call Johns Hopkins Hospital." But she learned nothing about Mrs. Honeywell's brother from this source, either. No one matching his description had been admitted.

The sisters were extremely disappointed. As they stood discussing the whole situation, the front door of the hotel opened and Mrs. Harland walked in. She said she had returned the car to the garage and talked to the owner about the hole in the gas tank.

"Did the man have any idea who might have put it there?" Jean asked her.

"Yes, he did. It had to be someone who was around the garage within an hour of the time we took the car. Just before that, the owner filled the tank and left the car in front of the gas pump. Then he went off for a cup of coffee."

Jean broke in excitedly, "The car wasn't parked by the pump when we found it!"

"Exactly. Someone moved the car, so it would stand over a pile of sand. Then he punched a hole in the tank. The gas that leaked out was soaked up by the sand. That's why we didn't notice anything was wrong."

"Who is the suspect?" Louise queried.

"The only person the owner saw around is one of the oystermen in town who isn't too trustworthy."

"Did you learn his name?" Louise inquired.

"Yes. It's Jake Maxwell."

The Danas dashed into the street and down to the docks, determined to find out where Jake Maxwell was now. They were told he probably was oystering out in Tom's Cove. Louise and Jean decided to question him later if possible.

"What reason would a man we don't know have for delaying our trip?" Jean asked her sister with a puzzled expression, as they walked back toward the hotel.

Louise was thoughtful for a few moments, then said, "The way I figure things out is this: Michael Fales has learned we're trying to help the Honeywells and hired Jake Maxwell to stop us. Delaying our trip with a punctured gas tank was a way to keep Kim and her mother in Salisbury a long time while waiting for us.

"In the meanwhile, Fales, using the name Tenney, had sent the cable to Claude Cooper, expecting that he would instantly get in touch with the Honeywells and discourage them from coming to Chincoteague. All this proves to me that Captain Forsythe *is* still alive."

"I agree with you one hundred per cent," Jean said. "And I suggest we keep on looking for the captain along the shore of Assateague Island."

Her sister heard the remark, but at the same time was looking toward the street where a taxi was just letting out some passengers. "The boys!" she exclaimed, and flew to the porch of the hotel. "Ken!" she called, as a tall, slender youth with blond hair rushed to greet her.

"Louise! Boy, it's good to see you again! Do you realize that I haven't seen you all summer? Between my being at camp and your European trip—"

By this time a second boy, dark and somewhat shorter, and with a lively twinkle in his eyes, rushed up to greet Jean. "Golly, I began to think one of those European princes was going to keep you over there forever!"

"Hi, Chris!" Jean laughed merrily, then she and her sister said hello to a third boy as he stepped onto the porch. Louise added, "Ronny, I'm so glad you're here. I'll call Doris right away."

It was not necessary to do this. Doris had heard the greetings from the second floor and had rushed down to extend her own welcome. The three boys registered, then carried their luggage to a bedroom assigned to them. They quickly changed into sports shirts and shorts and rejoined the three girls, who had waited on the porch.

"All ready for Pirate Island!" Ken announced.

Louise glanced at her wrist watch. "I'm afraid that it's too late to go there today. It's a long ride from here. Instead, I'll bring you up to date on a mystery we're solving."

After all the facts and the theories had been told, the boys gaped in amazement. "It's sure complicated," Ronny remarked. "I'll stick to digging for treasure."

"I'll tell you what we can do now," Jean proposed. "Let's go find Sam Everett. He's the man who was recommended to us as a pilot. He owns a small cruiser and a dinghy with an outboard motor."

It did not take long to find Sam Everett. He was a ruddy-faced man of about fifty, with a large bald spot in the center of his reddish-blond hair. He smiled pleasantly, but the Danas decided that his firmly set jaw indicated he was a person who would stand no nonsense and that he could become very angry if provoked too far.

"He'll be handy to have around if we should meet Michael Fales," Jean told herself.

The young people arranged to leave with him in his cruiser at nine the next morning. They were ready by eight-thirty. As they said good-by to Mrs. Harland and Mrs. Honeywell, the women cautioned them to be careful.

"I'm sure that I'm in good hands," said Kim, who was thrilled to be included with the three couples.

It was a gay, happy group that left the hotel and

walked to the dock. Chris, who was carrying a boxed lunch prepared by the hotel chef, said, "What's in here, anyway? Rocks? This sure is heavy!"

"That means we won't starve," Doris replied, giggling. "Here in Chincoteague they serve such large portions of food that after every meal I feel as if I'd gained five pounds!"

As the trip got under way, the boys asked many questions of both the girls and their pilot. Noting their interest in the territory, Sam Everett suggested that he take them on an indirect route to Pirate Island, so they might see Mills Island.

"It's just off the mainland coast," he said. "There used to be lots of wild turkeys and deer on Mills. Maybe you'll see some of them."

After a moment Chris remarked, "To tell the truth, I'd like to get right to Pirate Island. We fellows have been thinking for a long time about trying to find the treasure that's supposed to be buried there and we want to look over the place."

Sam Everett grinned. "A bunch of Jim Hawkinses, eh? All right, we'll go to Mills on the way back."

After a while he called attention to a shoal some distance ahead which was barely visible under the water. The young people were intrigued by a flock of small, brown-backed birds which seemed to be resting on top of miniature waves. They sat side by side, in a line nearly half a mile long.

"What kind of birds are they?" Louise asked.

"We call 'em tads. You probably think they're sitting on the water. Actually they're standing on the shoal. Watch what happens as we run closer."

Presently the birds heard the boat's motor. They became frightened and took off in flight. But their way of doing this was a new sight for the Northerners. The tads rose straight into the air, then the line divided exactly in half. One group went east, the other west.

"It would be interesting to know why they do that," said Doris.

"I never heard anybody tell why," Sam Everett replied. "It might be for protection."

A little later the cruiser reached the group of barren islands in the Pirate group and at Doris' request stopped at the central and largest one.

"This is where I found the English coin," she told Kim and the boys.

The young people took off their sneakers and waded ashore.

"I hope," said Chris, as he gazed at the ground intently, "that we fellows are going to find a lot of old Spanish pieces of eight! Jean, would you like a bracelet of pirate coins?"

Jean twinkled. "I'd love it. And now that you've mentioned such a gift, you'd better carry through and see that I get one!" she teased.

When Louise suggested that they eat lunch on the tiny island, the boys waded back to the boat to

bring the food ashore. Sam Everett said he preferred staying aboard, so his share of the picnic
lunch was taken from the enormous box and
handed over.

Jean passed the various wrapped packages to her
friends. As Ken unwrapped one, he exclaimed,
"Fried chicken! *Um!* That goes right to a man's
heart!"

"Really?" Jean grinned. "I thought it was going
to your tummy!"

Banter and much hilarious laughter accompanied
the eating of the delicious lunch. During part of
the meal Ken had been peering toward the shore of
Assateague about half a mile away.

"What's the long think for?" Louise teased him.

"I have an idea," Ken replied, "but I want to
look at a map before I spring it on anybody."

Just then Sam Everett called that if the young
people had finished eating, he would like to get
started back. They cleaned up and waded out to
the cruiser.

The pilot set his course toward Mills Island. As
the sight-seers reached it, they saw wild geese flying
above the woods.

"What a pretty sight!" Kim exclaimed.

Suddenly they heard a gunshot from the island.
"Someone must be after those geese," Ronny surmised.

When none dropped, Sam Everett said, "I don't

think so. And for anything but marsh birds, this isn't gunning season."

Just then a wild turkey flew squawking from among the trees and lighted on the beach. There was another shot and the bird fell dead.

The pilot shouted angrily, "I can arrest people shooting out of season. I'm going ashore and find out who's doing that!"

He brought his boat closer to the beach and turned off the engine. He asked the boys to take care of the cruiser during his absence. Then he quickly donned hip boots, waded to shore, and disappeared among the trees.

The next second, to the young people's horror, a bullet whistled over their heads!

CHAPTER VIII

The Cave-In

INSTANTLY the young people dashed into the cabin of the cruiser and fell to the deck.

"Good night!" Ronny cried out. "I didn't know there were snipers around here!"

"We didn't, either," said Doris, her voice trembling. "Oh dear, let's get out of this place!"

Jean reminded her that they could not leave until Sam Everett returned. "We can't just run off with his boat," she said.

Doris heaved a great sigh and said no more. The shooting had stopped and the young people wondered if Sam Everett had caught the rifleman. But their pilot did not return.

Finally Ken stood up and poked his head out of the rear of the cabin. "Everything seems to be quiet now," he stated. "But you girls had better stay inside."

He stepped to the afterdeck and the other two boys followed. As minute after minute went by and Sam Everett did not return, the group became worried about his prolonged absence.

"I'm afraid that something has happened to him," Louise said. "I think we should go ashore and find out."

The boys offered to do this, but Kim protested that she did not feel the girls should be left alone. "There might be more shooting!"

"I'd like to join in the search," Jean spoke up.

"I would, too," Louise added.

It was finally decided that the Danas would go with Ken and Chris. Ronny would stay with Doris and Kim to guard the boat.

"Watch your step please!" Doris begged the four as they climbed over the side of the craft.

They splashed through the water, stepped onto the shore, and began tramping through the woods. They took turns calling out Sam Everett's name but received no answer.

"I don't like this at all," said Louise.

The searchers looked carefully for footprints but could find none. Sam Everett seemed to have disappeared into thin air.

"What'll we do? Go back to the boat?" Jean finally asked.

At that moment she and the others heard a boat's motor start up in the distance, and they saw a figure dart suddenly from behind a tree and sneak off.

"That man looked as if he had a beard!" said Jean tensely. "He could be Michael Fales!"

Ken and Chris were already running after the suspect. They called to him to halt but the fleeing man paid no attention.

Louise and Jean joined the chase. For some time the four friends were able to keep the person ahead in sight. But presently he disappeared among the trees. His pursuers plunged after him but soon came to a dead stop. They had reached a junction of three paths.

"I think he went this way," Ken guessed, pointing, but Chris shook his head. "I'm sure that it was this other direction."

"Perhaps it doesn't matter," said Louise. "The main thing is, we haven't found Sam Everett. I vote we return to the shore and see if he's there."

The others agreed and they made the long trek back through the woods.

The boys called Sam Everett's name time after time, thinking he might be lying injured somewhere. They all listened intently, in case he could reply only weakly. But the boys' cries were not answered.

"I'm sure that he went back to the shore," Chris stated.

"I wonder if that was our boat we heard starting up," Jean said.

"Maybe we're marooned!" Chris spoke up. Then, with a broad grin, he added, "Ken, that wouldn't be so bad, would it, being marooned with two detectives?"

"What makes you think I'd stay?" Jean asked, tossing her head.

In another few minutes they reached the shore and both girls cried out, "Our boat is gone!"

Chris began to grin again. "What did I tell you?"

"Do be serious," Jean begged. "There's nothing to prove that Sam Everett took the boat and that he isn't still in those woods injured."

Chris sobered. "You're right. And since you want to take a dim view of the whole thing, try this: maybe our friend Sam has been kidnapped!"

"Oh, stop it, you two," Louise begged. "Since the boat is gone, let's go back into the woods and make another search for Mr. Everett."

The two couples once more began to search. Suddenly they were electrified by hearing another shot.

"Where did that come from?" Ken asked quickly.

"Over there." Louise pointed toward the north.

The four wondered if the shot had been fired at some turkey or deer, or was meant to scare away intruders.

"Or it might be a signal," Louise said. "Do you know if Sam Everett was carrying a pistol?"

"No, I don't," Ken answered, "but it won't hurt to find out where the shot came from."

Quickly but warily the Danas and their companions hurried through the woods toward the spot from which the shot had come. They saw no one, but presently heard a voice call out, "Help! Help!"

"Somebody *is* in trouble!" said Chris, and started to run.

"Be careful!" Jean warned him. "This might be a trap!"

Ken called out to him that he thought the four of them should stay together, so Chris waited for the others to catch up. Then they stalked ahead stealthily.

"Help! Get me out of here!" a man's voice was pleading.

The sound was very close now, and in a few more seconds the searchers came to a pit. It was about eight feet deep and at the bottom of the cave-in stood a man. He was a stranger to the four young people, and they knew from the fact he had no tattoo on his arm that he was not Michael Fales.

"Thank goodness you all came!" said the man, who looked to be about thirty years old. "I've been in here since last night and nobody heard me call."

"We'll have you out in a jiffy," said Ken.

He lay on the ground and reached down into the hole to help the trapped man. The spongy earth at the edge of the pit began to give way and Chris yanked Ken back in a hurry.

"We'll have to think up another way to get this man out of here," Ken stated. While he was mulling this over, he called down, "What's your name and where are you from?"

"I live right on this island," the man replied. "Name's Kurt Welch."

He explained that he had been roaming the woods, looking for a certain kind of medicinal herb. Suddenly the ground had given way and he had tumbled into the pit.

"Were you shooting?" Louise asked him.

"No. I'm not carrying a gun. This isn't the hunting season."

"Do you know who was firing the shots?" Ken queried.

"No, I don't. He didn't come near me."

Ken suddenly snapped his fingers. He said that he had figured out how they could rescue Mr. Welch. "I'll try again what I did before, but this time, Chris, you hold my feet."

The boys lay down and the experiment began. Ken had just reached to the trapped man's up-stretched finger tips when Welch suddenly jumped up and grabbed the boy's hands. The unexpected pull of added weight made Chris lose his hold. Ken plummeted down into the hole!

"Oh!" the Danas cried out.

Chris stood up, shamefaced. Then, to the on-lookers' horror, the bottom of the pit caved in still more. Ken and his companion were now twice as far below the surface as Kurt Welch had been before!

"Are you all right?" Louise called down fearfully.

Ken assured her that they were. But to his intense surprise Kurt Welch, instead of apologizing for having made their predicament worse, turned on the boy furiously.

"Some help you are!" he growled, and came at Ken with fists swinging.

Ken stood his ground. "Cut that out!" he said sternly, and caught the fellow's wrists in a viselike grip. "We've got to keep cool heads."

Welch glared for a few seconds, but finally calmed down. Meanwhile, aboveground, Louise's mind had been whirling. They must do something to rescue the men and do it fast! The floor of the pit might give way even more!

"Maybe the boat has returned by this time," she said to Chris and Jean. "I saw a long coil of rope in the cabin. Suppose you two run back to the shore and get it if the boat's back."

"What about you?" Jean asked.

Louise leaned forward and whispered, "I don't entirely trust Kurt Welch. I'd prefer staying here."

CHAPTER IX

A Disgruntled Passenger

CHRIS BARTON was reluctant to leave Louise Dana alone in the isolated woods. But she insisted upon staying, whispering that at least she could keep Ken company. Also, Louise added, if Kurt Welch again became belligerent, she would run for help.

"I can take care of myself," she assured Jean. "Besides, you and Chris won't be gone long."

When Jean and Chris reached the shore, they discovered to their dismay that the cruiser still had not returned.

"Maybe we could signal some other boat and borrow a rope," said Jean hopefully.

A few moments later they saw one in the distance. It seemed to be coming their way. With a feeling of relief the couple shouted and waved frantically. But suddenly the boat swerved in another direction.

"Oh dear!" Jean cried out.

"I guess the pilot didn't hear us because of the roar of his motor," Chris surmised.

"This is dreadful!" Jean said, walking nervously up and down the shore. "We must figure out some other means of rescue. Maybe there are matted honeysuckle vines that are long enough and strong enough to be used as a ladder."

Chris said he feared that at this season the vines might be drying out and be too brittle. "Anyway, it might take us a long time to find some."

"We'd better go back," Jean urged.

But at that moment Chris cried out, "Look! Here comes our boat now!"

The cruiser was emerging from what was apparently a cove in the island and in a few minutes reached Jean and Chris. To their delight Sam Everett was aboard and uninjured.

"Boy, are we glad to see you!" Chris called out.

"We're sure glad to see you, too," said Ronny. "Where did you go?"

Before they had a chance to answer, Doris asked fearfully, "Where are Louise and Ken? They haven't been hurt?"

Quickly Jean explained what had happened and asked Sam Everett for his coil of rope.

"I'll come along with you," the pilot said. "I want to talk to this man Welch myself."

He asked that the three young people on the boat stay there to guard it. "Don't let any strangers aboard!" he directed.

Ronny nodded and Sam Everett went ashore with the coiled rope swung over his left shoulder. Chris led the way.

"Did you catch the man with the rifle?" Jean asked the pilot.

"No, I didn't," Everett answered. "I got a fair look at him, though, and I'm pretty sure he was that fellow who calls himself Mr. Smith from London. As soon as he saw me, he started to run. I went after him. He did fire one shot, not at me, but into the air. I think he was just trying to frighten me and keep me from following. But I didn't aim to let that scare me."

Everett went on to say that he had trailed the man to the shore and was just in time to see him jump into a speedboat hidden in a cove and race off.

"I ran back to my own boat and we took off in the same direction that Smith had. We chased him until he deliberately ran aground and disappeared near the shore."

"Where was that?" Jean asked.

"A deserted section of the mainland over the Maryland border," Sam Everett answered. "The nearest telephone I knew about was at George Island Landing. So I decided to go there and notify the Maryland police."

Sam Everett explained that first he had examined Smith's speedboat and found a rifle in it. Before calling the police he had telephoned the Chincoteague man who had rented Mr. Smith a boat, and learned that the abandoned craft was indeed the same one.

"I'll tell the Maryland police to let you know when they find him," Sam Everett promised.

Chris then told their pilot about the man whom the young people had chased in the woods. "We thought he might be Smith, but he couldn't have been. I wonder why he ran away from us."

"Perhaps he was Jake Maxwell," Jean suggested, and explained to Sam Everett why they suspected that he had put the hole in the gas tank of the car they had rented when going to meet the Honeywells.

"I wouldn't put it past him," the pilot replied.

By this time Jean, Chris, and the pilot had reached the pit. Louise looked relieved, but said it had been very quiet during Jean and Chris's absence.

"I guess that's because Mr. Everett trailed the man with the rifle," Jean said, and quickly told her sister the whole story.

"It still doesn't explain the last shot," said Louise. "That bullet must have been fired by Jake Maxwell."

As Chris and the pilot got ready to lower the rope, Jean took her sister aside. "If that man Mr. Everett chased was Michael Fales, this island may be his hiding place," she declared.

"But he won't dare come back," Louise prophesied. "I wonder where he'll turn up next."

"I suggest that we ask the police to shadow Jake Maxwell. He may lead them to Fales." Louise nodded her approval.

The girls walked back to the pit. Everett and Chris were holding one end of the rope and leaning far back to counterbalance the weight on the other end. Louise and Jean peered over the edge of the hole and saw Ken coming up, hand over hand.

Soon he reached the top and stood up on solid ground. "Boy, am I glad to be out of that prison!" He stretched his arms far to the sides as if to illustrate his sense of freedom.

As Sam Everett and Chris leaned back on the rope once more, Ken whispered to them, "I don't fully trust Kurt Welch. I tried to find out more about him and he used a lot of double talk. I think you ought to make him prove his story that he lives here on the island."

"That's a right smart idea," Mr. Everett agreed. "We'll make him go in the boat with us to wherever he lives."

He had scarcely finished speaking when Kurt Welch's head appeared at the rim of the cave-in. As he stepped up, and let go of the rope, he muttered, "Thanks."

Without another word he started to move off. Sam Everett caught him by the shoulder. "Not so fast, son. We want to ask you a few questions."

"What about?" Welch's eyes darted suspiciously from one face to another.

"For one thing," Mr. Everett said, "we think you know more about that hunter than you're telling. Who is he?"

"Oh, all right. I'll tell you. I don't really know who he is, but he said his name was Smith and he came from London. Showed up at my house a few times to buy some eggs. I keep chickens."

"Then he's staying on the island?" Jean asked.

"I don't know. I think he has a boat, but I never saw it."

Once more, Kurt Welch started to leave the group. Again Sam Everett stopped him. "I think it would be a good idea for you to prove your story," he said sternly. "We'll take you home."

"I live a long way from here," Welch told them. "At the other end."

"Mills Island is privately owned," said Sam. "Aren't you trespassing?"

"I have special permission," the man muttered.

"We'll take you to your place in our boat," the pilot said firmly. "Come on."

Kurt Welch looked very much annoyed and eyed Everett malevolently. But the next second he seemed to realize that he had no choice. He shrugged and said, "Okay."

He was made to march in the center of the line, as the group picked its way back to the shore and

went aboard. The unwilling passenger was introduced to Kim, Doris, and Ronny. He barely
nodded, then walked the length of the afterdeck,
stepped over the railing, and squatted down in the
narrow space that formed the curved stern.

"Let him sulk," Sam Everett said.

"Yes," Jean added. "He didn't act very grateful
for being rescued."

As the engine started and drowned out any low
conversation, Doris whispered to the Danas, "Tell
us everything that happened! Don't leave out a
word!"

All the young people clustered in a group just
back of the opening to the cabin. They became so
intent on the story that no one even glanced at the
man about whom they were talking. By the time
the recital ended, Sam Everett was rounding the
end of the island. He was close to shore.

"Ask Welch where we should stop," he called
out.

Louise was first to turn around to speak to the
man. The next moment she gasped!

"He's gone!" she cried out.

CHAPTER X

A New Treasure Spot

EVERYONE on the cruiser turned around and stared disbelievingly at the vacant spot where Kurt Welch had been lounging.

"Oh, he must have fallen overboard. Maybe he drowned!" Doris said fearfully.

"It's not deep enough here for a man to drown," Sam Everett assured her. He throttled his motor and gazed up and down the shoreline. "Guess that's our man way over there." He pointed. "When no one was looking, he dropped off the boat and waded ashore."

The pilot gritted his teeth and an angry flush spread over his face. "I was pretty stupid not to think he might do that."

"Please don't blame yourself," Louise spoke up. "You had to steer the boat and watch where you were going. The rest of us should have kept our eyes on Mr. Welch."

Kim smiled sweetly at them all. "Let's not cry

over spilled milk," she said. "You are all doing this for me and Mother and Dad and Claude. Please don't let Welch's escape worry you."

The girl's sensible suggestion broke the tension. Nevertheless, Sam Everett declared, "I'm going to stop at Sinnikson—a little place on the mainland. Got an errand to do there anyhow, so I may as well call the Maryland police. I want to check that Kurt Welch's story, and find out if he does live on Mills Island."

After going nearly seven miles, the pilot pulled into an inlet where some oyster boats were tied up. Back from the dock stood a low, yellow house which Sam Everett said was Leon Sparrow's restaurant and that his wife was an excellent cook. He suggested that perhaps his passengers would enjoy some of the good food that was served at the place.

"And there's something interesting here connected with the oyster industry," he remarked. "After I make my phone call and we all have something to eat, I'll show you."

They all jumped ashore at a small pier, tied the lines, and went to the restaurant. The menu looked so intriguing that it made the young people suddenly ravenous. They all ordered fried-oyster sandwiches and fresh peach shortcake. But Sam Everett stuck to his favorite dish, ice cream.

"I sure feel better now," said Ken, as they finished eating and he got up to pull out Louise's chair. "Falling into that hole gave me an appetite. First it made me sleepy; then it made me empty. How do you figure that out?"

"Why, that's easy," said Chris. "You plunged right into a yawning cavern."

Ken gave his friend a playful shove. "Worst pun I've heard since the last one you made."

The whole group went outside. Sam Everett led them along the dock until they came to a machine which looked very much like a cement mixer, except that the revolving barrel was made of wire. It was filled with oysters and a workman standing nearby held a hose which carried a swift stream of water.

"He's washing the screw borers off the oysters," Sam Everett explained. "Those pesky little enemies attach themselves to the oysters. You'll find it right hard to believe, but within forty minutes they can bore clean through the shell. Then they begin to suck the oyster and of course that kills it."

"If the oysters are already dead, why do you bother to wash the screw borers off them?" Jean asked.

"Those little critters got right smart appetites," Sam Everett answered. "The minute they get through with one oyster, they attack another."

The visitors noticed that the wire mesh was small enough to keep the oysters from being pushed through, but large enough to eject the screw borers. One by one they flew out and dropped to the ground. Everett went over to pick one up and brought it back to show his passengers. The grooved shell, which looked like a cornucopia at one end, was only an inch long.

"It's just the color of an oyster," Louise remarked. "And really kind of pretty."

Sam Everett nodded. "But just the same, the little parasite is a mean devil."

He went on to say that when the hosing was finished, all the oysters would have to be examined for holes which the screw borer had made. The bad oysters would be discarded and only the untouched ones taken to the shucking house and canned.

"And now we'd better go," Sam Everett urged.

After the cruiser was out in the bay again, Ken asked the pilot if there was a marine map of the area aboard. Everett pointed to a locker in the cabin. Ken opened it and pulled out a large government map. After unrolling it, he commented:

"This is just what I wanted."

Ken studied it for some time, then flattened the map out on the deck for the others to study.

"You see this Pirate Island group?" he said. "They're a fair distance from the shore of Assateague. It's my idea they may not have been here at the time the old pirate buried his treasure."

"Sounds reasonable," Sam Everett commented.

Ken went on, "The way shoals are formed here, I think maybe what's now part of the Assateague shore may have once been an island."

"Very possible," the pilot agreed.

"In the reading we fellows did," Ken continued, "we found that many people have been digging for the treasure but no one has yet located it."

"Yes, go on," Louise prodded her friend, as he paused, gazed at the map, then ran a forefinger along the shoreline of Assateague opposite Pirate Island.

"I think it would be foolish to dig on any of the present islands in the Pirate group. I have a strong hunch that we should concentrate our efforts on Assateague."

Ronny slapped his friend on the shoulder. "Pal, you've really got your brain working. I'm beginning to agree with you."

Chris, too, said he thought the idea had merit.

Sam Everett grinned. "I wish you all a right smart amount of luck," he said. "So far as I know, not a soul has thought of such a thing before."

"How early can we start tomorrow?" Ken asked him.

"That depends upon how early you eat breakfast," the pilot replied, his eyes twinkling. "I'm sure that you don't want to get up at the crack of dawn like these watermen around here do."

"No, not that early." Ken laughed. "We have to wait until the stores open and do some shopping for camp equipment and supplies. Let's make it ten o'clock."

Chris added that he would like the girls to go along and help the boys set up camp. "And we

"I have a hunch that the old pirate buried
his treasure here," Ken said.

want you to visit us every day and bring fresh supplies."

"Aye, aye, sir. Any more orders?" Jean asked, pretending to be miffed.

"Oh, sure. Bring some of that good fried chicken and oyster stew and—"

"Hold on!" said Jean, still pretending to be severe. "Campers are supposed to eat canned ham and beans—and, for you pirates, hardtack."

Everyone laughed, and the boys struck ludicrous poses of begging for mercy. When the merriment died down, Ronny asked, "While we boys are digging for the treasure, what are you girls going to do?"

Louise replied quickly, "Continue our hunt for Captain Forsythe."

"Oh, I'm glad to hear that," Kim spoke up.

Sam Everett asked if the girls were familiar with running small power boats. Upon hearing that they all were, he said, "Days when I can't take you on your search, I'll lend you the dinghy with the outboard motor. She's a great little boat. If you get in shallow water, you just haul up the motor and do a little rowing. You can travel around in water less than a foot deep and not scrape bottom."

"Fine!" said Louise. "We'll be glad to take it."

She looked at the pilot, intending to ask a few questions, but noticed that he was intently watching a speedboat coming in their direction and did not want to disturb him.

"Fool!" she heard him mutter under his breath.

The oncoming craft was going at terrific speed, its nose completely out of the water. Sam Everett moved to the right in order to pass the speedboat. But just before the other pilot reached the cruiser, he deliberately cut across Everett's path.

Everett swung his wheel hard to the left, hoping to avoid a collision!

CHAPTER XI

Deep-Sea Prize

THE DANAS and their friends, sure a collision was imminent, closed their eyes to shut out the sight. Each second they thought the next would bring a splintering crash.

When nothing happened, they all opened their eyes and looked about them in amazement. The speedboat which had crossed their path was now some distance away.

A little shakily Louise said, "Mr. Everett, you're —a—marvelous pilot! How did you ever avoid the other boat?"

"Well, no thanks to that crazy fool Jake Maxwell!"

"Jake Maxwell!" Jean exclaimed. "You mean that the man in the speedboat is Maxwell?"

"None other."

"Then let's chase him!" Jean urged. "We think he can help us solve the mystery!"

Sam Everett shook his head. "No sirree, miss. I

aim to get you folks back to Chincoteague safe and sound. No telling what Jake Maxwell will think up next. But I'll tell you what I'll do. Soon as we get to Chincoteague, I'll notify the local police about him."

"And the Maryland police too," Doris suggested. "I don't ever want to see that man again. The sooner he's found, the better I'll like it."

When the pilot let his passengers out at the dock, he said that he would meet them at ten o'clock the following morning. During the evening he telephoned them at the hotel to report having contacted the police.

"While I was talking to them, I picked up some other news," he told Louise, who had taken the call. "I learned that Kurt Welch really does live on Mills Island and keeps chickens. The police quizzed him about Mr. Smith, but couldn't find out anything more, so I guess Welch was telling the truth. Well, I'll see you in the morning."

But when Louise and Jean and their friends assembled for breakfast the next day, the desk clerk came to tell them that Sam Everett had changed his mind. "He phoned about half an hour ago. Said he was very sorry, but he won't be able to take you out in his boat today. Some emergency came up that he has to attend to."

The treasure hunters were disappointed, and discussed trying to find another man with a boat to carry them to Pirate Island.

"Oh, we can wait until tomorrow," Ken spoke up. "It'll give us time to do our camp shopping and look around Chincoteague a bit."

"I have a better idea," said Chris. "Who wants to go deep-sea fishing?" Then, before anyone answered, he admitted he was not so interested in catching fish as he was in using the skin-diving equipment he had brought along. "Especially if I could look at a wreck," he added.

"That's a great idea," said Ken, who also had diving equipment with him.

After breakfast the boys consulted Mr. Wolfe. The amiable man highly recommended a Captain Wien, who had a very seaworthy ship and liked young people.

"That's a perfect combination," Louise said when the boys told her this later.

"We'll leave in just one hour," Chris said. "Tell the others, will you?"

The girls and boys met on the porch of the hotel and set off together for the waterfront. Captain Wien's boat proved to be very neat and fully equipped. Spaced at intervals around the edge of the deck were fishermen's swivel chairs with leather sockets at the base to hold the end of the fishing poles. From fore and aft of the top of the good-sized cabin long metal rods stretched out like giant antennae.

"They're for special trolling," Ronny explained to Doris, who looked puzzled.

Captain Wien was a stout, good-natured man with a deep, rolling laugh. He greeted the young people with a broad grin and said he hoped they would come home with a good catch.

"What kind of fish are running this time of year?" Ken asked him.

"Channel bass, sea bass, weakfish, porgies, croakers, fluke, cobias. Take your pick!"

"I'll take cobia," Kim spoke up, giggling. "I never heard of it. Is it good to eat?"

"Oh, yes. Cobia is a favorite with my wife."

A crewman cast off and Captain Wien started the engine. He headed down the narrows and out the inlet. The young people watched the scenery for a while, then went to talk to the captain.

Ken told him about the boys' having brought two sets of diving equipment. "Would there be any chance of our investigating a wreck?" he asked hopefully.

"Why, I think so. There are plenty of them around. I'll pick one that isn't so far down."

"Thanks," said Ken. "How soon will we come to it?"

For answer, Captain Wien threw back his head and laughed heartily. "Thought you boys wanted to fish. What do you aim to do with the young ladies? Let them do the fishing?"

Ken flushed slightly at the needling and said hastily, "Oh, we'll fish too."

Without Ken seeing him do it, the captain gave

the four girls a long, slow wink. Then he drawled, "I always have reckoned the womenfolk ought to be considered, whether it's eating, or fishing, or skin diving."

"Why—of course," Ken agreed. "What are you driving at, Captain?"

"Well, now, son, I'd hate to think these young ladies here wouldn't have a chance to see a wreck as well as you boys."

"Why, yes—sure," Ken said, a bit flustered. "You mean we can take turns diving down to the wreck?"

"There wouldn't be time for that," Captain Wien replied. He seemed to be enjoying Ken's discomfiture. When he thought he had teased the boy long enough, he said, "I have a proposition to offer. First we'll go fishing. The two of you who catch the biggest ones by four bells will be elected to put on the skin-diving equipment and look at the wreck." This time he grinned at the girls' disappointed expressions. But he seemed to guess that they had not brought their swim suits and announced, "I always carry a mess of bathing togs for the ladies."

The girls burst out laughing, and Jean said, "I'll take you up on the challenge, Captain. First prize to Miss Jean Dana!"

Louise pursed her lips. "Maybe I or one of the other girls will hook the biggest fish."

"Of course Jean will get the prize," Chris said gallantly. "She'll know just how to lure him."

Louise put both hands over her ears. "I can't stand another joke that bad," she said. "Anyway, we're using live bait and not lures, aren't we, Captain?"

Captain Wien nodded and chuckled merrily as he gave his craft more power. It cut through the water at high speed for several miles. Then he slowed it down and finally throttled the engine, so that the craft was barely moving.

"Now we'll start trolling," he said.

He and his crewman helped the girls bait their lines with pieces of fish. The young fishermen sat down in the chairs, held the poles over the railing, and let the bait down into the water.

"Oh, what's that strange-looking thing floating toward us?" Kim asked suddenly.

All eyes turned to see a gigantic black mass with sides that were pointed and shaped like wings. Captain Wien told them that the creature was a manta ray and should be avoided. He put on power and moved his boat some distance from the ray.

The fishermen were quiet for a while, then Louise exclaimed, "I have a bite!"

The crewman hurried to her side to see if he could be of assistance. Louise reeled in slowly, then feeling a tug, let the line out a bit, but finally hoisted her catch into the air.

"Good for you!" Captain Wien called out. "That's a right smart fluke, miss. Must weigh five or six pounds."

Louise beamed. "I dare you all to equal this!"

She had hardly spoken when Ronny hauled in a channel bass, which when weighed proved to be over ten pounds.

Doris looked at the fish, then suddenly asked, "Do we have to eat everything we catch?"

A deep-throated chuckle came from Captain Wien. "I reckon there are plenty of folks who would like to have them. Any you don't want the hotel chef to cook, you just let me know."

The fishing contest went on for some time. Kim did not hook a cobia, but she did bring in a two-pound porgy which she declared she would eat for her supper.

"Help!" Jean called out a moment later. "I must have a ton of concrete on the end of my line!"

The crewman rushed to her chair and steadied the rod which was bending at a tremendous angle. Jean was using every ounce of strength to reel in her catch.

"It must be a whopper!" the man whistled. "Shall I help you?"

Jean gritted her teeth. "If I'm going to win that chance to see the wreck, I guess I'll have to pull this monster in alone."

Although it was a struggle, she managed to bring her catch to the surface and land it on the deck.

"Wow!" Chris cried out. "A channel bass—and a beauty!"

The hook was removed from the fish's mouth and he was weighed. Jean's eyes bulged as she watched the marker go up and up to twenty pounds!

"Congratulations, miss," Captain Wien said. Then he laughed. "Guess I'd better go break out the bathing suit for you."

Some time went by before any more fish were caught. Doris pulled in an eight-pound weakfish, but Chris, to his chagrin, had had no luck so far. The captain suggested that they give up for a while and have some lunch.

The fishermen got up to stretch and walk around the deck. Then the crewman served ham sandwiches, apples, and milk. He told the group there was plenty more food aboard if anyone wanted it, but they preferred the light snack.

While they were eating, Louise asked Captain Wien if he was acquainted with Captain Forsythe.

"Yes, I am. Do you know him?"

Louise shook her head and Captain Wien went on, "He's a fine man—one of the finest I've ever met—and a skilled ship's pilot."

Jean leaned forward. "Then Captain Forsythe wouldn't be apt to make a mistake and cause a collision when he was piloting a vessel?"

"Never!"

Kim asked Captain Wien if he knew where Captain Forsythe was. "I understand he hasn't been around here for six months," she said.

"That's what I've heard. I can't figure where he could have gone, unless—" Captain Wien paused and looked out over the horizon. "Unless he shipped out on some sailing vessel just for old times' sake."

The young people exchanged glances. Here was a possible new clue! They did not say any more about the matter to Captain Wien and in a little while went back to their fishing.

Chris had no sooner settled himself in his chair than he felt a sharp tug on the line. Hardly daring to believe his good luck, he did not tell anyone else. In a moment Chris realized the fish was going to put up a vigorous fight.

"But I don't intend to lose him!" the boy thought determinedly.

By this time Captain Wien saw that Chris had a prize catch on the end of his line and he walked over to watch. The battle proved to be a tough one, but Chris stuck it out and twenty minutes later gave a whoop as he landed an enormous sea bass.

"It's bigger than mine!" Jean cried out.

She was right. The fish weighed twenty-five pounds.

After Chris had received the group's congratulations, he said, grinning, "Captain Wien, how about heading for that wreck now? It's just four bells."

The skipper smiled and nodded. He turned his

cruiser south. A little later he announced, "We're coming to a section where there's a shoal. Down along one side of it you'll find what's left of a wrecked ship. If you want to put on your diving gear, now's the time to go down and take a look. Just watch out for sharks. They're in these waters and sometimes they get nosy."

Hearing this, Doris begged her friends not to go, but Jean and Chris promised to be careful and went to change into swim togs. Then, with the others helping, they adjusted the fins and donned the helmets and their tanks of oxygen.

Chris went down a rope ladder which hung over the boat's side and Jean followed. In a few moments the two disappeared beneath the surface.

The couple was fascinated as they gazed through the water at a myriad of fish of many varieties darting around. Down, down, the two swam and presently came upon the wreck. It had once been a sailing ship, and now only the rusted metal parts remained.

"It would be fun to have something from this ship as a souvenir," Jean told herself. She swam close to an anchor and began to dig in the sand which surrounded it.

As Chris came over to see what she was doing, Jean's fingers touched something. Excitedly she tried to loosen the object and motioned to Chris to help her.

Together they uncovered a small metal water

pitcher. Chris grinned and nodded, pointing upward.

Carrying the heavy pitcher between them, they
rose to the surface. Jean climbed the ladder first,
as Chris held up their prize for the others to see.
Then he followed.

While the divers removed their equipment, Captain Wien brought a cloth and began to wipe off
the pitcher. It was black and covered with barna-
cles. In a few moments the group could see that
it was made of copper. Small patches of the original
silver plating still remained.

"How absolutely exciting!" Kim said enthusiastically.

They all noticed that the neck of the pitcher was
plugged up. Jean's eyes sparkled. "This may mean
there's something valuable inside! Let's find out!"

CHAPTER XII

Double Cross

THE PLUG filling the neck of the antique pitcher was as hard as concrete. Captain Wien produced a small sturdy fish knife and Chris began to chip out the plug. Ten minutes later the last bit of it fell away.

"Be careful!" Ronny warned, as Chris started to upend the pitcher. "There may be liquid in there and you'll spill it."

Chris shook the pitcher. There was no sloshing sound, but something inside rattled. Jean grabbed her sweater from the back of a fishing chair and spread it out on the deck.

"Drop our treasure in here," she suggested.

Chris knelt and very gently tipped the pitcher, holding the lip directly over the sweater. A moment later several tiny packages, all wrapped in fragile dark-red silk, fell onto it.

"I can hardly wait to see what's inside the package!" Louise said excitedly.

Feverishly Jean began to unwrap one. There were three layers of the silk. From them she lifted an exquisite porcelain medallion with a woman's head on it.

"How astounding!" Kim cried out. "You've really found treasure!"

"We won't have to go to Pirate Island after all!" Jean said gaily as she started to unwrap a second article.

The boys remained silent, staring in amazement as a bracelet was revealed. By the time all the packages had been opened, Jean's sweater held a collection of old coins and various kinds of antique jewelry, all of it attractive but not enormously valuable.

At last Ken spoke up. "The big treasure's still up by Pirate Island, remember," he assured the others. "Up there we're going to find doubloons and pieces of eight!"

Jean made a face at him. "You're just jealous," she said. "I dare you to go down to *this* wreck and find something."

Ken turned to Captain Wien. "Is there time?"

The skipper looked at his watch. "I could give you half an hour," he replied.

"Then let's you and I go, Louise," Ken urged.

Louise needed no second invitation and quickly put on a bathing suit and Chris's skin-diving equipment. She and Ken swam down to the wreck but could find nothing worth bringing to the surface.

Finally they came aboard and changed into their fishing clothes again.

Meanwhile, Captain Wien started the return trip to Chincoteague. After they docked, Kim insisted upon keeping her porgy. Chris and Jean proudly claimed the two prize channel bass. The young people gratefully gave the rest of their catch to Captain Wien.

As they reached the hotel, Doris exclaimed, "Mr. Everett!" The pilot was seated on the porch. Now he rose and came toward them.

"You sure caught a pair of whoppers!" he said. "The biggest I've seen lately."

Doris told him they planned to share the fish with the other hotel guests, and he thought this was a wonderful idea. Then he declared, "Our lines got right smart fouled up this morning."

"What do you mean?" Louise asked him.

Sam Everett amazed the group by telling them that he had not telephoned early that morning to say he could not take the young people to Pirate Island.

"You didn't!" Louise cried out. "Then who did?"

The pilot shrugged. "Somebody who heard us making plans for the trip double-crossed us," he said, frowning. "After I waited nearly an hour for you folks, I walked over here to find out what the trouble was."

The Danas and their friends were alarmed by

this latest turn in the mystery. Finally Louise stated, "Im sure of one thing—Captain Forsythe must be somewhere in this area and we were so close to finding him that somebody stopped us from going on another search."

"Well, he won't stop you again!" Sam Everett declared. "Barring rain tomorrow, we'll make the trip. When I found out you weren't coming with me today, I did a lot of other jobs, so I'll be free in the morning."

"Great. We'll meet you at ten," said Ronny.

As Mr. Everett went up the street, Kim and Chris hurried to the hotel kitchen with the fish and were told it would be "cooked to order." They rejoined the group and everyone continued to discuss the latest development in the mystery. Doris pointed out that it contradicted Captain Wien's theory of Kim's uncle having shipped out on some sailing vessel.

"I'm so confused." Kim sighed. "Where *can* Uncle Tracy be?"

Excusing herself, she hurried upstairs to talk to her mother about the latest development. The others continued their conversation.

"I didn't want to say this while Kim was here," Jean spoke up, "but I'm afraid Captain Forsythe may be a prisoner of Michael Fales!"

"How horrible!" Doris burst out. "I'm glad that you didn't mention it to Kim or her mother."

The boys were up early the next morning to buy

their camping gear. Then at ten o'clock the entire group met at the dock.

Sam Everett, a can of metal polish in one hand, was vigorously rubbing the railing of his cruiser. "Good morning," he called cheerfully. "Before we cast off, I want you to meet an oysterman who knew Captain Forsythe well. He has something right interesting to tell you."

Eagerly the Danas and their companions boarded the cruiser. Sam Everett waved toward a man standing on an oyster boat moored next to his own craft.

"Folks, I want you to meet John Doolittle. John, these young people here would like to find the captain."

John Doolittle, a tall, lanky man, acknowledged the introduction, then said, "Captain Forsythe and I were great friends. I miss him. Sorry he went away. I figure it's not fitting to talk about other folks' business, so I never said anything like I'm going to tell you. But when Sam here asked me if I had any idea where the captain went, I changed my mind."

As John Doolittle paused, Louise inquired, "And you do have an idea?"

The oysterman took several seconds before answering, "You folks may think this sounds like a tall story, but I'll tell it to you for what it's worth."

As his audience listened intently, he said that one day Captain Forsythe had seemed very preoccupied and had finally startled John by asking a peculiar question.

"Captain Forsythe said to me, 'John, do you know of any place around here that's rumored to be haunted?' When I asked him what he meant by that, the captain said, 'I mean a place where nobody ever goes, because they think it's haunted.' "

Kim Honeywell was staring at John Doolittle. "What did you tell him?" she queried excitedly.

"I told the captain there were plenty of little inlets and lagoons along the shore of Assateague, especially the bay side. I've been caught a few times up around there myself. When it's dark and foggy and the wind's sighing in the trees, it sure seems like those places are haunted."

The Danas and their friends exchanged glances. Here was the best information they had yet received! Apparently, for some reason, the captain wished to stay in some reputedly haunted place in order not to be disturbed by intruders. But why?

"Can you tell us any more?" Kim begged.

"I'm afraid not, miss, but I sure hope you find the captain."

Kim thanked the man for the information, then Sam Everett cast off.

Instantly Louise hurried to his side. "May we please trail the dinghy today? I'd like to search in some of the inlets and lagoons where the cruiser can't go."

"Glad to take her along," Sam Everett agreed.

He asked the boys to tie the lines again while he went for the small boat with the outboard motor. He was gone for several minutes but finally the waiting group heard a *put-put* and presently their pilot appeared with the dinghy. Its painter was secured to the stern of the cruiser and Sam Everett jumped aboard.

He cast off, then set a direct course for Pirate Island. On the way they saw many flocks of brants flying over the shoals. At times the birds would come down to rest or catch fish in their bills.

"They're a pretty kind of geese," Louise remarked.

"And good eating," Sam told her.

During the entire trip the Danas watched the shoreline of Assateague intently. When they reached the spot where the boys were going to camp, Louise heard Ken say to Chris, "Since Sam isn't in a hurry today, do you suppose he'd lend us a hand? The more help we get with the digging, the quicker we'll find the treasure."

"Suits me," Chris replied.

This conversation gave Louise an idea. She went up to Sam Everett and asked, "While you and the boys are unloading the gear and setting up camp, may we girls take the dinghy and do some exploring? We'll meet you back in Chincoteague."

"That'll be all right," Sam agreed. "Just remember to haul up the outboard motor whenever you get into real shallow places."

"I'll remember," Louise promised. "Thank you."

She walked to the stern where the other girls were seated and told them about her plan. "Wonderful," said Jean. Doris and Kim, too, were enthusiastic.

As the girls were about to set out, Doris called to the boys, "You'd better have one part of the treasure dug up before we meet again!"

"We'll try to fill your order, ma'am!" Ronny called back, grinning.

Louise was seated in the dinghy's stern, controlling the tiller and the speed of the motor. She ran the little boat in and out of several small bodies of water, but there was no sign that Captain Forsythe was staying near any of them. No boats were hidden and they saw no shacks or tents to indicate human habitation.

As the girls were entering another small cove, Doris pointed ahead. "Look at those luscious huckleberries. I didn't know they could be picked so late in the season. They must be a second crop."

Kim looked worried. "You'd better be sure they are *huckle*berries before you eat them, Doris," she warned. "Some berries are poisonous."

Louise had already turned off the engine and hoisted it out of the water. She ran the boat ashore and the four girls got out. Before they had a chance to investigate the berries, they heard a faint but shrill neighing cry from some point ahead.

"What's that?" Doris asked.

"I'm not sure," Louise replied, "but I once heard an injured pony make just such a sound. Anyway, let's find out what it is."

The girls pushed their way through rank grass and bushes, with a tree here and there. The neighing grew louder as they approached the woods.

"Oh, look!" Jean cried out. "The poor thing!"

Just ahead of them was a large thicket of thornbushes. Caught among them and neighing pitifully was a young colt.

"Oh, we must help him get out of there," Louise exclaimed sympathetically. She darted forward, with Jean at her heels.

As they reached the colt, Doris suddenly screamed, and she and Kim dodged behind a large pine.

"Louise! Jean! Look out!" Doris yelled. "A stallion's coming! He'll trample you!"

At Doris' scream, Louise and Jean turned. Their eyes widened in horror. A black stallion, his nostrils dilated with fury, was galloping full speed toward the girls!

CHAPTER XIII

Dashed Hopes

DESPERATELY the Danas looked for a means of escape from the stallion charging toward them. Instinctively they began circling the thornbushes in which the colt was trapped.

"Maybe we can keep him at bay," Jean gasped to her sister.

But the enraged stallion was not to be easily fooled. Neighing shrilly and rearing, he plunged around the thicket after the two girls.

"Now he—he thinks we're trying to take the colt!" Louise cried breathlessly. "Jean, we'll have to run for it!"

"All right. Let's watch our chance."

For what seemed an eternity, the girls raced around and around the thicket, the horse pursuing them full tilt. The terrified colt, still trying to get free, gave another pitiful whinny.

At this, the stallion stopped, stretched his neck

among the thornbushes and nipped the youngster on the rump.

This was just the interruption the Danas needed. Quick as lightning they dashed across the tall grass to where Doris and Kim were huddled behind the tree. To the girls' amazement and relief, the stallion paid no further attention to them.

His shrill calls had brought the mother of the colt running to the scene. As the Danas and their friends watched, the mare and the stallion backed up against the thornbushes, making a small opening between them. In an instant the imprisoned colt dashed out and skittishly bucked and reared, enjoying its freedom.

"That's cute," said Louise. "But what a scare!"

"I was never more frightened in my life!" Doris exclaimed weakly. "I was positive that stallion was going to injure you and Jean."

The Danas were pretty shaken themselves. They were good horsewomen and used to temperamental ponies, but they had never had any experiences before with wild ones!

"Let's go!" Kim urged. "My knees have started trembling all of a sudden. I'm not even sure I can make the trek back to the boat."

Louise put an arm around the English girl. "You'll be all right in a few minutes. My own knees don't feel too steady."

The girls made their way to the shore and sat

down. For several minutes they relaxed without talking.

Finally Louise said, "Ready for some more exploring?" and the others nodded.

Louise left the small cove and started the dinghy south once more. She wound in and out of the many indentations of the shoreline without any of the girls finding a clue to indicate that Captain Forsythe was hiding in the area.

Finally Kim gave a great sigh. "I wonder if we'll ever find Uncle Tracy," she said woefully.

"Don't give up hope," Louise told her with an encouraging smile. "We've only begun to investigate all the hidden coves and lagoons."

Kim smiled in return and the search went on. Presently, as Louise turned into another small body of water, Kim sat up very straight. She pointed. "Isn't that a shack over there?" she asked excitedly.

Louise guided the dinghy in the direction Kim had pointed. They were so intent, looking ahead for what might be Captain Forsythe's hideaway, that no one noticed how shallow the water had become.

Suddenly the engine stopped. Louise groaned. Had she ruined it?

"Oh dear!" she said, and swung the engine up out of the sandy muck. "Jean, will you take one of those oars and shove us into deeper water?"

Her sister grabbed one oar and Doris the other.

In a few moments the dinghy had been pushed out of the shallows.

Louise let the outboard down into the water and called out, "Wish me luck!"

She started the engine. There was a sputter, then it died. She tried again, with the same result. Louise was worried. She and her friends must not be stranded all night in this wild, isolated place with no chance to notify Doris' parents or Mrs. Honeywell.

Determinedly Louise examined the motor. "Maybe the spark plugs got wet," she murmured, and wiped them thoroughly with a dry rag.

She tried the starter once more. No response. "You're not wishing hard enough," Louise told the other girls, trying to remain cheerful.

Again she studied the motor. This time Louise adjusted the carburetor setting. Hopefully she used the starter. The engine coughed a couple of times, then started up with a steady roar.

"I guess our rooting and your magic touch did the trick!" Jean sang out, and everyone heaved grateful sighs.

Kim said that if the girls were willing she would still like to go back and investigate the spot where she thought she had seen the shack. Louise agreed. This time she turned off the engine and tipped it up. The girls used the oars to take them toward the shore.

"There's marshy ground in front of the place you

pointed out, Kim," said Jean. "What say we get off here. It's sandy, and we can walk where it's dry."

"All right," Kim answered. She was the first one out of the boat and hurried along ahead of the others.

"Poor Kim!" Doris murmured sympathetically. "It must be awful having someone close to you just disappear."

"Yes, heartbreaking," Louise concurred, as the girls tramped after their English friend.

She was now a good distance ahead of the Danas and Doris, and suddenly they heard her cry out in fright. Rushing forward, they soon reached Kim's side. She was staring as if mesmerized at a long, black snake. The reptile was slithering away from a log onto which Kim had stepped.

"Is—is it poisonous?" the English girl asked fearfully, hesitating to proceed.

"No," Louise told her. "Black snakes are harmless."

Kim relaxed and all the girls moved ahead toward the spot where they thought they had seen a shack. Upon reaching it, the four stared in disappointment.

Then Jean burst into laughter. "Nature can be deceiving," she said. "There's no shack there at all. It's just the formation of those tree branches and vines that fooled us!"

The girls turned back toward the boat. As they reached it, Kim suggested that they give up any further searching for the day and go back to the hotel.

"You know I'm expecting Claude," she added happily, then looked up at the sky. "Besides, I think it's going to rain."

"You're right," Louise agreed. "The sooner we get back to Chincoteague the drier we'll be!"

Jean rowed the dinghy out to deeper water. Then Louise turned the outboard motor down and started it. The bay had become choppy and a strong wind was blowing. It was not long before the girls felt spatters of rain.

"I'm afraid that we're in for it," Jean remarked. "Look at those black clouds!"

"And not one of us with a raincoat!" Doris spoke up. "We're going to get soaked!"

Louise said she had noticed something black tucked under one of the seats. "Perhaps it's a poncho, which will help some."

Jean unrolled the black object. It was indeed a poncho and very large. The four girls huddled in the stern of the dinghy, which was so broad of beam that the prow could not upend. As they adjusted the poncho around them, like a hooded cape, the rain came down in a blinding torrent.

Louise was tense. "I hope I can get you all to Chincoteague without running aground on a shoal," she said worriedly.

CHAPTER XIV

The Rescue

THE TRIP toward Chincoteague was made in silence. Each girl strained her eyes to see through the deepening gloom and heavy rain, determined to assist Louise in every way she could.

Louise herself sat gazing ahead, her mouth set in a grim line, her jaw determined and her hands grasping the tiller hard. She moved it constantly, trying to figure out the depth of the water and keep on a safe course.

At last Jean spoke up. "I see buoys ahead! Now it will be easier, Louise."

"I hope so," her sister murmured. She found her way to the narrows and, guided by lights blinking on the water, at last came to Chincoteague. As she finally pulled up at Sam Everett's dock, the other girls hugged her.

"Louise, you're simply a wonder!" Doris sobbed with joy.

In a trembling voice Kim remarked, "I was terrified. Really I thought we'd never make it."

Jean said nothing; just gave her sister an understanding, appreciative look. Louise smiled back.

As the girls moored the dinghy, they suddenly realized that Sam Everett's cruiser was not there. "Do you suppose he's spending the night on the island with the boys?" Jean suggested.

Then, before anyone could answer, they saw the Everett boat approaching. The girls waved to the pilot, who drew up just ahead of the dinghy. In a few moments Sam Everett and all the girls were standing on the dock.

"Praise be!" he said, heaving a sigh of relief. "When I saw that storm coming in, I left the boys to their digging and tried to find you young ladies. I never figured you'd make it back here without a guide. You're right good navigators."

"My sister gets all the credit," Jean spoke up proudly.

Sam reached out and shook Louise's hand. Then he grinned. "If I had a medal, I'd pin it on you!"

Louise chuckled. "You people had better stop paying me compliments. I'll be so conceited I'll be asking Uncle Ned to let me run the *Balaska!*" Then she became serious. "Mr. Everett, will you be able to take us out tomorrow?"

"I'm afraid not," the man answered. "Sorry. But I'll tell you what. Since you're right smart at handling the dinghy, help yourself to her." Then he asked whether the girls had learned anything about Captain Forsythe.

"Unfortunately no," Jean told him. "But we want to continue our search in the morning." Her eyes twinkling, she wagged a finger at Sam Everett. "Don't you dare let it rain tomorrow!" The man laughed and said he would do the best he could for them.

Kim suggested that the girls go to the hotel immediately. "Claude may be there already."

The four friends said good-by to Sam Everett and hurried across the bridge. At the hotel they found that Claude Cooper had not yet arrived, so they went to their rooms to bathe and change their clothes.

Half an hour later, while the Danas were discussing the mystery, a knock sounded on their door. Jean unlocked it to find Kim standing outside, her face radiant.

"Are you girls dressed?" she asked.

"Yes."

"Then come downstairs with me and meet Claude. He arrived about fifteen minutes ago."

"Okay," said Jean, and the two sisters followed the English girl to the lobby.

Claude was seated there but instantly arose and introductions were made. The Danas liked the young Englishman at once. He was very tall, had a classic profile, a shock of blond hair, and blue eyes that were kind, yet had a mischievous twinkle.

"I hope you had a pleasant trip over here from London," Louise remarked.

"Yes, I did," Claude replied. "And I also enjoyed viewing the scenery on the drive from Salisbury to Chincoteague."

Claude Cooper immediately turned the conversation to Captain Forsythe. He was amazed to learn how much sleuthing the girls had done and declared he was sure they would locate Kim's uncle very soon.

"I'm not much of a detective," he said, "but I'll take on any tasks you offer me."

Louise told of the search proposed for the following day, then asked Claude if he had any suggestions.

"No indeed," the young man replied. "I'll just go along as a working passenger. By the way, Kim tells me three chaps are down here who are friends of you girls. I say, isn't it a bit risky for them, staying in such a desolate place without a boat?"

"Oh, they're well protected," Jean assured him proudly. "Chris is carrying a pocket radio sending set. He wouldn't be without it. If anything happens, he can call for help."

"A smashing idea," said Claude.

At that moment a man strode through the front entrance of the hotel and approached the group of young people assembled in the lobby.

"Can you tell me where I might find Mr. Claude Cooper?" he asked.

The English boy stepped forward. "I'm Claude Cooper."

"I'm glad I found you," the short, dapper man said. "And these are your friends who are trying to find Captain Forsythe?"

"Yes, we are," Jean spoke up.

The stranger introduced himself as Mr. Paul Scribner of New York. "I'm a guest on a yacht that's lying offshore. I came to Chincoteague in a small boat—I'm looking around here for a house to rent. I'd like to bring my family to the island on a vacation.

"While I was down at the dock I overheard a man asking another if he had seen Captain Forsythe lately." Mr. Scribner laughed. "If that wasn't a coincidence! Why, Captain Forsythe is the skipper of our yacht!"

"What!" everyone in the group cried out.

"To tell the truth," Mr. Scribner went on, "the captain doesn't want this known. So when I heard this conversation, I asked the man, 'Who wants to know this?' He told me that a group staying here at the hotel had been asking about the captain. Said that Mr. Claude Cooper was arriving from England and wanted to find out about the captain more than anyone else did."

"Why, that isn't true," Kim exclaimed. "The captain is my uncle. My mother and I are just as interested in finding him."

Mr. Scribner smiled. "I kind of figured something of the sort, from a couple of things Captain Forsythe said. Well, young lady, I'm going back to the yacht in the morning. How would you like to trail me?"

"That would be marvelous!" Kim told him. "I must run and tell Mother the good news."

Mr. Scribner said he must leave now and start house hunting. He would meet the group next morning at the other side of the bridge.

After Mr. Scribner left, there was a lengthy discussion with Mr. and Mrs. Harland and Mrs. Honeywell about the trip out to the yacht. It was finally decided that they would rent a large boat and all of them would go, since Doris' parents felt that the adults should accompany the young people.

"I think that's great," Louise told them. "You haven't had nearly so much fun as we have since you've been here."

Mrs. Harland smiled. "At least we haven't had as many exciting adventures. But perhaps tomorrow will change all that."

Mrs. Honeywell's eyes were moist. "It will be wonderful to see my brother again," she said.

After supper Mr. Harland and Claude went off together to see about renting a large, seaworthy cruiser. They were a little disappointed in having to settle for one only half as large again as Mr. Everett's boat. But its skipper, Captain Yuler, assured the men that his craft had been through many bad storms and proved her fitness.

"She may pitch and roll," he told them, "but she'll never turn over."

The next morning was cloudy and windy. Sam Everett came to the hotel to suggest that the four girls postpone their trip up the Assateague shore. "I thought after that storm last night, it would be a right pretty day today. But you can't tell about the weather hereabouts."

Louise told the pilot of their change in plans. "We've hired Captain Yuler's boat," she said. "I guess it won't matter what the weather does."

"I'm not so sure of that," Sam Everett replied. "But I reckon if you expect to see Captain Forsythe, you've got to make the trip."

At nine o'clock the whole group set off from the hotel. Captain Yuler was waiting at the dock, and Mr. Scribner, in a sleek speedboat, had his motor running and was about to start off. The others scrambled aboard the cruiser, which followed the smaller boat.

"Powerful engine in that speedboat," Captain Yuler remarked. "Enough to tear it apart."

As his own craft reached open water, he glanced uneasily at the sky and the ocean. Both looked angry and threatening. "We'll have to make a quick trip of this," the skipper told his passengers.

They could now see the yacht dimly in the distance. The speedboat was racing toward it at a clip which the cruiser could not attain. Captain Yuler frowned and set his jaw firmly. His own boat was bouncing over the rough sea, with tremendous wind-tossed clouds of spray breaking over the bow. By this time Mr. Scribner was out of sight.

"I guess he wants to reach the yacht before the storm gets any worse," Doris remarked.

Everyone kept his eyes on the yacht as the cruiser cut through the water at full speed. Captain Yuler picked up a pair of binoculars and handed them to Claude Cooper. "See if you can spot that speed-boat," he requested.

Claude took the glasses and trained them on the water ahead. Presently he reported, "I don't see it anywhere. And I say, I think that yacht is moving! And fast, too! By jove, I'm right!"

Captain Yuler grabbed the binoculars with his left hand, as he steadied the wheel with his right. After staring through the glasses for a moment, he said, "I can't figure this out. Mr. Scribner never had time to make that yacht. And it's not like Captain Forsythe to leave—he'd wait until all his passengers had come aboard."

"He certainly would!" Mrs. Honeywell exclaimed, shocked.

Louise and Jean held a whispered conversation, then Louise spoke up. "It looks as if Mr. Scribner's story was just a hoax to get us out here on a wild-goose chase."

"Then all this means," said Mrs. Honeywell, on the verge of tears, "that my brother is not on that yacht."

"I'm afraid so," Louise told her. "But please don't give up hope. The strongest clue we have had yet is that he went off to some hidden lagoon along the shore of Assateague. We'll find him!"

"Oh, I hope so—and soon!" Kim's mother said fervently.

Captain Yuler had circled and was heading back toward Chincoteague. The cruiser rocked and tossed. Each moment the wind grew stronger. Waves were mountainous and crashed over the boat. The sky had become so leaden that the land was completely blotted from view.

"This is like a hurricane!" Mr. Harland shouted above the roar of the storm.

Captain Yuler confessed that it was. "Most unusual in these parts."

The skipper ordered everyone to put on a life belt. As the passengers tried to keep their balance while donning them, a mountainous wave hit the cruiser, completely enveloping it. Water broke open the cabin door and poured inside.

The cruiser weathered the onslaught, but Captain Yuler radioed to the Coast Guard for help. The others were relieved to hear the answer that a rescue boat would start out at once.

Minutes went by, with the passengers becoming more and more panicky. Another giant wave hit them, tearing off the cabin doors. The receding water carried Claude Cooper with it, tossing him into the surf!

Kim screamed. The others gasped in horror. Mr. Harland grabbed a coil of rope and started outside the cabin.

"You'll be swept overboard too!" Mrs. Harland cried out fearfully.

At the same moment there was a resounding crash. Captain Yuler spun his wheel but the effort was useless. "We've hit a log!" he shouted.

The Danas knew the cruiser was helpless now. It was just a matter of time before she might be ripped apart.

Their next thought was that they must help Mr. Harland rescue Claude Cooper. Grabbing the framework of the doorway, they tried to steady themselves. Mr. Harland was kneeling on the deck, struggling to tie one end of the rope to the railing. The other end was already out in the water and the girls could see Claude making vain attempts to reach it.

At the same moment they became aware of a boat's shrill horn and heaved sighs of relief. The Coast Guard rescue boat!

Over his microphone Captain Yuler asked that the man overboard be rescued first. One of the coastguardmen, wearing a life belt and secured to the rescue boat by a line, jumped into the water and swam with strong strokes to Claude's side. Then, using a lifesaver's grasp, he supported the Englishman and both were drawn to the rescue boat.

"Claude's saved!" cried Kim, tears in her eyes.

In the meantime, the patrol boat had maneuvered upwind from the pitching cruiser. A rubber life raft, attached to a rope on the rescue boat, was lowered, with a coastguardman handling it.

The raft floated downward. When it was fairly close to the cruiser, its skipper tossed a coil of rope aboard. Captain Yuler caught it and dragged the bouncing raft closer. One by one his passengers,

Claude made a vain attempt to reach the rope.

then he, were taken off and transferred to the rescue boat. The next second there was a splintering crash and the once sturdy cruiser cracked apart.

Its skipper sat sad and silent on the deck of the

rescue boat as he watched his own little ship disappear beneath the waves. Those aboard the rescue boat tried to comfort him by saying the freak storm alone could be blamed for the wreck.

Louise and Jean felt that another and more sinister force had been largely instrumental in causing their predicament—an unscrupulous former convict, even now wanted by the English police for robbery. Michael Fales, alias Smith, had probably put Scribner up to the scheme of luring the unwary victims out to sea.

Claude Cooper, recovered from his shock, had the same thought. "I vow to get that beastly, low-down Fales!" he declared grimly.

By the time the rescue boat reached the Coast Guard station on Chincoteague, the harassed group had nearly regained their composure, although they were wet, cold, and uncomfortable. As they stepped ashore, Doris said to Louise and Jean:

"I'm worried sick about Ronny and Chris and Ken. I don't see how they could have escaped being injured in this terrible wind."

CHAPTER XV

Chasing an Enemy

THE BAD STORM in the Chincoteague area subsided in a very short time. The skies cleared and the sun soon was shining. The coastguardmen said the storm had moved out to sea.

The Danas and other passengers of Captain Yuler's wrecked cruiser told him how sorry they were about his loss and asked if he planned to replace the boat.

"Yes, and right quick. I'll get the insurance and buy a spanking new one," he replied. "Can't be without a boat."

When they reached the hotel, Doris mentioned the boys again. Louise put a reassuring arm around the girl, reminding her of Chris's short-wave sending set. "I'll contact the police to find out if any message came through."

Over the telephone she learned that the police had received no report from the boys.

Doris was still worried. "We must go to the Pirate Island area and find out for ourselves!"

"All right," Louise agreed. "Let's ask Sam Everett for permission to use the dinghy."

The pilot was not around the docks, so Louise came back and telephoned his wife. To her astonishment Louise learned that Sam Everett, worried about the boys, had gone to their camping spot himself to see if they needed help.

"I'll have Sam phone you the minute he gets home," Mrs. Everett promised.

Louise, Jean, and Doris went upstairs. Their flagging spirits were somewhat restored by hot baths, shampoos, change of clothes, and a delicious luncheon of oyster stew and broiled chicken.

It was late afternoon before the Danas and Doris heard from Sam Everett. But his news was cheering. He stopped at the hotel and smilingly reported that Ken, Chris, and Ronny were safe and in the best of health.

"But your friends had a right tough time of it," he went on. "A lot of their equipment was ruined, and supplies blown away. I was afraid something of the sort might've happened, so I fetched them blankets and some food.

"The boys," Sam Everett continued, "want you girls to come up to camp tomorrow morning and bring them new equipment and more food."

"Will you help us pick it out?" Jean asked.

Sam Everett said that he would be very glad to and would meet the girls the next morning at nine.

The following day he arrived at the hotel

promptly. The Danas and their young friends, after saying good-by to Mr. and Mrs. Harland and Mrs. Honeywell, set off for the stores.

The group divided. Doris, Kim, and Claude were delegated to buy the provisions, while the Danas and Sam made the camp purchases. The food shoppers finished first, so they joined the others at the place where the tent was being selected.

A decision had just been reached when everyone was startled by a tremendous roaring sound.

"Wh-what's that?" Doris burst out, frightened.

"I reckon it's a rocket launching over to Wallops Island," the proprietor replied.

As the roar continued, everyone in the shop except the owner rushed out to the street. A moment later the Danas and their friends heard a loud whine, followed by a *swoosh*.

"There it is. I see it!" Jean cried out.

All eyes watched as a long, slender rocket shot upward at unbelievable speed. Reaching a great height, it arced slightly, then headed due south. In a few moments it disappeared from view.

"I wonder if this one is headed for the moon," Doris spoke up, laughing.

Louise smiled. "I think only sounding rockets are launched here, to observe weather conditions."

Further speculation on the subject was interrupted by Claude. Grabbing Kim's arm, he said excitedly, "I think I just saw Michael Fales!"

"Michael Fales! Where?"

Claude did not wait to answer. He dashed past the group of stores and turned into the yard of an oysterhouse. As he sped on toward the docks, the girls raced after him.

When they caught up, Louise asked breathlessly, "Where did Fales go?"

"I don't know. He must be hiding some place around here. Let's investigate!"

A search began. Claude, the girls, and Sam Everett looked under the pier, in the docked boats, inside sheds, and in the oysterhouse itself. The man with a fringe of beard and his jacket collar turned up—whom Claude thought to be Michael Fales—was not found.

"I'm sure that man was Fales!" Claude declared. "The London papers were filled with pictures of him."

"When did you last see him in person?" Sam inquired.

The young Englishman said it was at the time of the accident to the *Sea Ghost*. "But I'll never forget his face. That's why I'm sure the man I saw was Fales. He looks older now, of course, but those penetrating eyes of his—as a boy they scared me out of my wits."

"Then you couldn't have been mistaken," Sam remarked. "Suppose I walk along the waterfront and keep my eyes open for this man. In the meantime, you young folks run back to the store and fetch your bundles. I'll meet you at my boat."

Claude and the girls hurried off to the store where they had left their packages. Claude completed the purchase of the tent, selected a small camp stove and a large lightweight jug, which the store proprietor filled with water. The young people started off. As they reached the far side of the bridge, they saw Sam Everett waving wildly for them to hurry.

"He must have seen Fales!" Claude exclaimed hopefully.

When he and the girls reached Sam, he pointed excitedly toward the center of the channel. "See those two speedboats?" As they nodded, watching one turn north, the other south, he added, "I think Michael Fales is in one of 'em. I couldn't be sure which one, because both men had their backs to me. But I did see they have dark hair, and jackets with the collars turned up."

Louise groaned. "We can't chase both those boats at once," she said.

Sam offered to go after the craft heading south toward the ocean. "Suppose you folks take the dinghy and chase the one that's going north."

The Danas and their friends needed no urging. As Sam Everett hurried off in his cruiser, they ran full speed to the dinghy and jumped in. Claude cast off, while Louise started the motor. As she headed northward, everyone was on the alert for a speedboat with a lone, black-bearded passenger.

After going some distance without seeing him,

Louise veered in order to pass close to a nearby oyster boat. Claude shouted a query to the man running it.

"Yes, I saw that fellow," the waterman answered. "Just keep goin' straight ahead and you'll find him."

Louise sent the dinghy forward at top speed, but they did not come upon the suspect's boat. Again Claude called out to a passing oysterman. He, too, had seen the person they thought might be Michael Fales. Those in the dinghy still had no luck in catching up to him. Presently they came upon a third oyster boat, but this man said he had not seen the speedy craft.

Kim sighed. "Michael Fales must have slipped into shore and landed some place."

"That would be too bad," said Jean. "We haven't the least idea whether he went to the mainland or to Mills Island or to Assateague. What do you think we should do, Claude?"

"Really, I'm at a loss to answer," the Englishman replied.

Doris interrupted to say that she thought they should give up the hunt for the moment and go on to the Pirate Island area to deliver the campers' supplies.

"Also," Louise added, "we may have been chasing the wrong man. Perhaps Michael Fales is in the boat Sam Everett is after."

With this thought in mind, the young people pushed on toward the camping spot, and half an hour later reached it. The three delighted boys gave cries of joyous welcome, and took the various articles which were either handed or tossed to them from the dinghy. Then the visitors went ashore.

After the boys had heard about their friends' terrifying experience on the ocean, Ken, Chris, and Ronny admitted that they had been pretty lucky by comparison. "Only lost our light equipment," Ronny told them.

"Our digging operations were ruined by the storm, though," said Ken. Then he grinned. "But just before the hurricane, we dug up this prize."

He put a hand into the pocket of his jeans while Claude and the girls waited expectantly to see what the treasure was.

CHAPTER XVI

The Phantom Ship

"A PIRATE's earring!" Louise exclaimed in astonishment, seeing the shiny two-inch hoop in Ken's hand.

"It sure is!" Ken replied proudly.

"And you dug it up here?" Claude Cooper queried, reaching out to take the treasure for a closer look.

Claude turned the earring over and over in his fingers, examining it minutely. "There is no doubt but that this is very old, and I never heard of any men but pirates wearing solid brass hoop earrings."

Ken beamed and urged that they all pitch in and dig. The campers had not brought enough tools to go around, so the entire group took turns using the ones they had.

For the next hour everyone worked very hard. The campers were brought up to date on the mystery and were sorry to learn Fales had escaped.

The ground became riddled with deep holes, some wider than others. The eager workers grew hot and tired. Nothing had been found but oyster and clam shells, and bird skeletons.

Then, suddenly, Claude called out, "I've struck something!" Grinning, he added, "Water!"

The others laughed, and Chris asked, "Is it fresh or brackish?"

Claude, whose head could barely be seen above the top of the hole, leaned down and tasted the water. "It's fresh—and good," he announced.

Louise stopped her work and looked toward him. "Then we'll have visitors," she said.

"What—or who—do you mean?" Claude queried.

"The wild ponies are always looking for fresh water holes," Jean told him.

"Great!" Ken slapped his forehead. "All we need now is a band of ponies to come and interrupt our work."

Jean suggested that they all take time out and have a picnic lunch from the provisions which had been brought to camp that morning.

"Good idea, if there'll be anything left for us fellows to use later," Ronny needled from his digging spot.

Cans of pressed beef were opened, and the meat spread onto slices of rich, buttered rye bread. Bottles of chocolate milk were taken from a pail of ice and uncapped. The weary treasure hunters sat cross-legged in a circle and ate the delicious picnic lunch, which ended with ripe bananas.

Suddenly Chris yawned. "Pardon me," he said. "It's not the company, just hard labor and a good meal. Anybody mind if I take a short nap?"

No one did—in fact, the entire group was glad to rest for a while. At three o'clock Claude Cooper looked at his watch. "I don't want to seem like a quitter—really I don't—but I think the girls and I should leave and do some more searching for Captain Forsythe."

"Of course," Ken spoke up. "It was swell of you all to come here. We'll look for you again tomorrow. You'd better save plenty of time this evening to get back to town, though."

Claude and the girls climbed into the dinghy and waved good-by. Louise offered to give up her job as helmsman, but the others shook their heads. Kim flashed her a smile. "Why should we change places with our best navigator?"

Louise grinned, and the boat purred along due south until the searchers reached the area where they had stopped hunting on their previous trip. Then Louise turned into the next inlet they reached. Every inch of the shore was scanned closely. Apparently no one was staying there.

About a quarter mile farther on, they came to another inlet. The entrance to this one was blocked by a battered tree trunk.

Kim leaned forward excitedly. "Maybe this is where Uncle Tracy is hiding! He might have put up this tree as a barrier to keep people out!"

Louise and Jean nodded. "But we could never move it without help," Jean told her, "and that gives me an idea. If your uncle did put this here, it means that he had help. And that in turn means somebody else knows his secret. If we can't find your uncle, then we should start looking for this other person."

"Yes," Louise agreed. "If there's a lagoon in there, maybe it has another entrance. Let's look."

She went on and in a little while did come to another inlet. This one was very narrow.

Kim said hopefully, "I wonder if this will lead us to my uncle."

Although the inlet was shallow, it was deep enough for the dinghy to proceed under power. But the little craft, with its noisy engine and talking passengers, seemed to have disturbed one of nature's rendezvous. Brants screamed overhead, while short-legged cranes rose in fright out of the marsh and flew off.

"This seems to be a birds' paradise," Doris remarked. "Do you suppose no one is staying here?"

"You mean not even Uncle Tracy?" Kim asked in disappointment.

"No, nor Michael Fales. Don't forget, we haven't found him yet, either."

"That's right," said Claude. "I'd temporarily forgotten all about that scoundrel."

The inlet twisted and turned. The engine on the dinghy had been working perfectly, but without warning it stopped abruptly. Louise, puzzled, looked at the fuel gauge. It registered half full. The throttle and spark plugs were all right. She pushed the starter. There was not a sound from the engine.

"What's the trouble?" Claude asked, leaving his seat beside Kim and walking back to Louise.

"I don't know," she replied worriedly.

The young Englishman began tinkering with the engine, but could not get a spark. Jean took a turn. She had no better luck.

"I wish I could help," said Kim, "but I don't know a thing about motors."

The group sat in gloomy silence for several minutes, wondering what they could do. Then Doris arose and made her way to the stern. Hardly realizing what she was doing, the girl bent over the engine and pushed cautiously at a couple of loose wires, then used the starter. The engine burst into life! No one was more surprised than Doris.

"Bully for you!" cried Claude. "The wires from the spark plugs to the ignition coil had become disconnected!"

Kim said, "You're a magician!"

Doris laughed, then her face sobered. "It's going to be dark soon. We shouldn't go any farther. We might get stuck again. Let's come here tomorrow."

The others, too, felt that it might be safer to return to the bay. There they could summon help, if necessary, should the engine give out completely.

"I'll back out," Louise said.

But she remembered to her dismay that this was not possible. There was no provision on the motor for reverse gear.

"We'll either have to row back, or go ahead to find a spot large enough for me to turn around."

"Let's go ahead!" Jean proposed enthusiastically. "The engine seems to be working all right now. And we can always row out if it gives us any more trouble."

"I'm game," said Claude, and Kim nodded.

Doris looked dubious, but she knew they had little choice. So the dinghy went forward. The Danas, Doris, and the English couple were silent for a while, their eyes taking in the thickly tangled undergrowth along the banks. A sense of utter isolation came over them.

"This would be a perfect place to hide," Kim murmured presently. "I have the strangest feeling that Uncle Tracy is somewhere near here."

The thought spurred the others on. It was now becoming dusk and wisps of fog were swirling about. Nevertheless, no one wanted to give up the search. The mist in the air grew thicker as they advanced. Then, suddenly, they came to a lagoon.

"Thank goodness," said Doris. "Now we can turn around."

But Kim begged, "Before we go, let's get out and do a little exploring along the shoreline."

Claude and Doris agreed to accompany her, and the three stepped onto the ground, which fortunately was not marshy. Louise and Jean decided to remain in the dinghy to guard it from any unfriendly person who might be lurking.

As the sisters waited, darkness and a deep fog settled over the place like a velvet curtain. But a moment later the gloom was penetrated by a flash from the Assateague lighthouse. Now the scene was illuminated approximately every forty seconds by the great beam.

There was not a sound until Jean suddenly gasped, "Look!"

Louise raised her eyes and gazed straight ahead unbelievingly. Across the fog-shrouded lagoon, with the light directly on it, was a full-rigged sailing vessel! It seemed to be suspended in mid-air above the water!

CHAPTER XVII

Mysteriously Detained

THE DANA girls stared ahead in complete fascination. As the beam from the lighthouse vanished, they waited tensely for it to reappear and reveal again the weird vessel which seemed to be sailing through air.

"There it is!" Louise murmured in awe, as the suspended ship was once more lighted up in the fog. "Jean! I think I see a man on deck!"

"I thought so too," her sister said, as the beam swept past. The sisters waited, as if hypnotized, for the scene to be illuminated again.

Thirty seconds later the great light swung in their direction. The Danas were aghast.

"It's gone! The ship's gone!" Jean cried out.

"A phantom ship!" Louise added. "A ghost!"

The girls continued to stare at the spot, thinking they might see the floating vessel again. But the lighthouse beacon now showed only mist and trees where the Danas had witnessed the strange apparition.

"What was it?" Jean asked her sister. "If you hadn't seen that ship too, I'd think I was a little balmy."

"I can't fathom it," Louise replied. "But I'd like to investigate that spot."

"What spot?" Jean said. "You can't investigate the air!"

By this time Doris, Kim, and Claude had come rushing back to the dinghy, and climbed in hurriedly. All three said they too had seen the startling sight.

Doris urged, her voice shaking with fright, "Let's get out of here as fast as we can. This lagoon certainly *is* haunted!"

Kim and Claude were white-faced. "Shivers are going up and down my spine!" Kim said.

Claude sat staring ahead. In a halting voice, full of emotion, he murmured, "Th-that ship! It was just like—just like the old *Sea Ghost!*"

"The *Sea Ghost!*" Jean exclaimed. "You mean the ship that Captain Forsythe once skippered?"

"Yes."

"Did you think you saw a man on deck?" Louise spoke up. "We did."

"No. Really?" Claude responded. He, Kim, and Doris looked startled.

"But of course there couldn't have been a man, since it was only a phantom ship," Kim remarked.

"Yes," Claude Cooper agreed, "but it looked exactly as if a picture of the *Sea Ghost* had been thrown on some gigantic screen."

The Danas could give no logical explanation of the specter ship, but they did remind the others of the story they had heard that Captain Forsythe had been looking for a haunted lagoon.

"Maybe we've found his hiding place at last," Louise suggested.

"That still doesn't explain the ghost ship," Doris stated. "We can't do any more sleuthing tonight. I suggest we come back tomorrow."

Claude said he hated the thought of giving up the search, but added, "We'll not be able to see very far ahead in this fog, so we could run into real danger here."

Kim and the Danas realized it was all too true and agreed to go back.

Louise started the engine. To her delight, it sputtered, caught, then ran smoothly and steadily. She swung the dinghy in a wide arc, and with Claude holding a large flashlight in the bow, Louise headed out of the inlet.

Her skill as a helmsman was brought into full play, and she performed admirably. Only once during the nerve-racking trip through the narrow inlet did the dinghy's passengers receive a scare; that was when the propeller churned up sand. But Louise quickly stopped the motor and lifted the engine up. When it was safe to do so, she put the propeller back into the water and the journey out to the bay was completed without accident.

Louise laughed in sheer relief, even though there was still fog and several miles to go.

"I feel as if this has all been a weird dream," Doris declared with a tremendous sigh, and her friends said they felt the same way.

Presently the group became aware that there were many craft on the water. Furthermore, boat whistles were tooting and horns blowing.

"What's all the commotion about?" Kim asked.

"I haven't the least idea," Louise replied.

Jean thought the boats were trying to signal someone. "Or," she added, "maybe they're looking for lost persons—like us for instance."

The young people noticed a small cruiser coming in their direction. As it drew closer, they recognized the boat. Sam Everett was at the wheel!

"Well, hallelujah! We've found you!" he cried out from the side window of his cabin. "You think it's fitting for you folks to scare the wits out of everybody in Chincoteague?"

"As bad as that?" Jean called back.

"Sure was. We got a water posse together—been hunting for you an hour. Where've you been?"

"In ghostland," Jean replied. Then, seeing that Sam Everett obviously thought she was being flippant, Jean told him the story of the phantom ship.

Sam scratched his head. "You're not joking?" he asked.

"It's all true," Claude Cooper put in seriously. "Most unbelievable thing I've ever seen. You can jolly well bet we're going back there tomorrow and investigate."

"I'd like to go along with you," Sam Everett said.

Conversation now turned to Michael Fales. Sam Everett reported that the man he had chased had proved to be someone else. Sam was disappointed to learn that the young people had failed to apprehend the man they had been trying to catch, but he said cheerfully:

"The police or some of us are bound to catch up with Fales sooner or later."

The pilot then suggested that the dinghy's passengers come aboard the cruiser and tie the smaller boat to it. One by one the young people climbed up. None was more relieved than Louise. Although she had said nothing, she had not relished the idea of guiding the others back to Chincoteague in the fog.

A warm welcome awaited the group when they reached the hotel lobby. Everyone was exceedingly relieved to see the young people safe and unharmed. In their honor Pop struck up a lively tune on his banjo.

The starved travelers were served an appetizing

hot meal of clam chowder, steak, and homemade apple pie. As they ate, Louise and Jean told the story of the phantom ship to the Harlands, Mrs. Honeywell, Mr. and Mrs. Wolfe, and Nat Steelman, who had come to the hotel to see the sisters and their friends. The Chincoteagueans were astounded, but could give no explanation.

Plans were made by the Danas and their young friends to start off the next morning with Sam Everett directly after breakfast. They would try solving the mystery and continuing the hunt for Captain Forsythe.

Louise arranged with the hotel chef for a lunch to be packed. As she went to pick it up the next day, Claude announced that he and Kim would like to take a few minutes to do an errand in town before leaving.

"It will not take long," the English girl assured her friends. "Claude and I will meet you at the dock."

The Danas and Doris, carrying the packages of lunch among them, strode leisurely to the waterfront and across the bridge. They said good morning to Sam, then went aboard his cruiser and sat down. After a while Louise looked at her wrist watch. Half an hour had gone by since Kim and Claude had left the hotel.

"Where did your English friends go?" the pilot asked.

"We don't know exactly," Louise answered.

After another ten minutes elapsed, Jean began to frown. "Surely they wouldn't hold us up this long. I have a horrible hunch something has happened to Kim and Claude. Let's go look for them."

"But where?" Doris queried.

Jean Dana proposed that the three girls separate and do some questioning. Doris could go from house to house, and Louise from store to store.

"I'll take the waterfront," Jean offered, adding, "We'll return here within fifteen minutes to report to one another."

Sam Everett smiled. "Don't I get a job?"

"You'd better stay here in case Kim and Claude do come back," Jean suggested.

When the searchers met again, Doris reported no success. Louise said that one of the shopkeepers had identified the English couple as customers who had purchased books with a Chincoteague background an hour before, saying they wanted to take them back to England. The proprietor had not noticed where the couple had gone.

Jean, in her trek along the waterfront, had learned nothing, but just then an oysterman drew up not far from the Everett cruiser. On impulse, Jean hurried over to him and asked if he had seen a young couple in a boat.

"Not by themselves," the waterman answered. "I did see a man and a girl with an older fellow.

The three seemed to be having an argument."

"What did this older man look like?" Louise questioned quickly.

"I didn't notice much, except that he had sort of a fringe of black beard."

The Danas and Doris looked at one another in alarm. They were sure the people in the speedboat were Kim, Claude—and Michael Fales!

"Where was the boat headed?" Jean cried out.

The oysterman pointed toward the ocean. Louise, Jean, and Doris grew tense and their hearts pounded. All feared that Kim and Claude had been abducted by the former first mate of the wrecked *Sea Ghost!*

CHAPTER XVIII

The Shack on Stilts

"WE MUST find that speedboat at once!" Jean exclaimed. "Mr. Everett, will you take us out right away?"

"You're pretty sure your English friends are the passengers in it?" Sam asked. "That may be a real speedy boat like the one Mr. Scribner had, and we probably couldn't catch up to it now."

Louise said she was unable to figure out any other reason why Kim and Claude had disappeared. "Let's get started!" she begged. "Every minute counts!"

"Yes," Doris put in. "Please! We can try."

Sam Everett, convinced, set his jaw and sent his cruiser plowing through the water. Louise picked up binoculars from a bench in the cabin, walked to the prow of the boat, and trained the glasses on the water ahead. There was no sign of the speedboat. She reported this to the pilot.

"We'll keep after 'em!" the man said determinedly.

Louise continued to gaze through the binoculars. They were very powerful and she could see objects in detail along either shore as well as on the open water. There was still no sign of a speedboat with three people in it.

As the moments passed, the three girls became more and more discouraged about the fate of the English couple. Doris, who had grown particularly fond of Kim, was on the verge of tears.

"I see a boat!" Louise called out suddenly. A few seconds later she added, "But it's empty!"

Sam Everett's brow puckered. "I don't like the sound of that," he said grimly. "Are you sure nobody's in it?"

Louise gazed steadily at the speedboat which was bobbing about in the waves a half mile from the mouth of the Chincoteague inlet. She told the others that there was definitely no one in the boat.

Doris began to cry. "Oh, Kim and Claude may have drowned!" she wailed.

The Danas were puzzled. Surely Michael Fales would not have let himself drown, even if he had intended that Kim and Claude would. But where was the black-bearded man?

As they neared the abandoned speedboat, Louise and Jean gave startled cries.

"Kim and Claude!" Louise gasped. "They're in the bottom of the boat—tied up!"

"Glory be!" Sam exclaimed. "They're alive and okay."

Within five minutes the cruiser was alongside the helpless couple. Louise and Jean jumped into the speedboat and quickly untied the ropes which bound the prisoners.

"Oh, you adorable people!" Kim exclaimed as Claude helped her into the cruiser. "How did you ever find us?"

"We'll tell you later," Louise replied. "What happened to you two?"

Claude expressed his gratitude to his rescuers, then launched into his story. He and Kim had finished their errand at the shop in a few minutes, and since it was too early to meet the others at the dock, they had strolled along the waterfront.

"Suddenly I saw Michael Fales," Claude went on. "He was sitting in this speedboat, huddled over, as if he did not want anybody to recognize him. I ordered the scoundrel ashore, so I could talk to him."

As Claude paused, Kim took up the story. "Michael Fales paid no attention to us, even when Claude called him by name. Quick as a wink he started the motor. We were desperate because we knew he was going to escape, so Claude and I jumped into the boat with him."

Claude resumed the story. Fales had whizzed full speed out into the channel. A heated argument had ensued between the two men, with Fales denying that he was the person they sought.

"But to prove it," Claude continued, "I pulled

up his shirt sleeve and there was the telltale tattoo—M.F.

"Fales got nasty. He said he was not going to give himself up to the police, even though he did admit being wanted for robbery in England, and by the United States authorities because he had entered this country illegally."

Kim spoke up to say that Fales had persistently denied knowing anything about Captain Forsythe. "We asked him why he had come to Chincoteague, but he refused to answer us."

Claude then said he had tried to overpower Fales, so that he might steer the speedboat back to Chincoteague. But the struggle grew so violent that the boat had rocked dangerously, and Kim had pleaded with them to stop fighting.

The English girl shuddered. "And the worst part was still to come."

Kim explained that another boat had approached. But to her and Claude's horror, the man in it, instead of coming to rescue the couple, had turned out to be a local henchman of Fales's.

"He was that same Jake Maxwell who nearly ran into us the other day," Kim added. "He's a wicked person. All the time Michael Fales and he were tying us up, he kept laughing loudly, making bad jokes, and slapping us on the shoulders. Oh, he's perfectly horrid! I hope the police find him soon and put him in jail!"

"We all do," said Louise indignantly. She turned

to Sam Everett. "What do you think we should do about the speedboat?"

Their pilot thought that it should be returned to Chincoteague, and suggested that one of the young people run it. Claude offered to do so and climbed back into the craft. Kim said she would accompany him. Sam led the way and in a little while they were back in Chincoteague.

"I reckon," the islander said, "you all want to call the police. And also, the way news travels around here, I guess Mrs. Honeywell has heard by this time about the two of you being missing. Maybe it would be fitting for you to run up to the hotel and relieve her mind while I gas up my boat."

The Danas and their companions followed his advice. Within half an hour the five were back.

Sam Everett smiled at them. "Are you all calmed down now?" he asked.

"Aye, aye sir!" Jean answered gaily for everyone, and Claude added, "We're ready to tackle that haunted lagoon."

"I'll consider it right smart if you can find an explanation to that spook ship you folks saw last night," Sam declared.

"We're certainly going to try hard," Claude replied resolutely.

Their pilot had tied the dinghy to the stern of the cruiser. When they reached the narrow inlet leading to the lagoon, he said they would transfer to the small boat.

Before anyone could move, Doris made a request. "Mr. Everett," she said, "I'd feel a whole lot safer if we could get the other boys to come with us." Blushing a little, she added, "They'll be extra protection and we may need it."

Jean objected. "We have two men already. I think that's enough, Doris. Anyway, let's not waste any more time getting to the lagoon."

Kim too was eager to start the search, but agreed with Doris that it might be safer if the other three boys were around. Sam Everett settled the matter by his offer to go alone in the cruiser to bring the campers.

"Your friends and I can walk along the shore of this little inlet up to the lagoon," he said. "I noticed that the boys have boots, same as I do. We'll all put them on."

As soon as the girls and Claude had transferred to the dinghy, Sam Everett set off. Louise, at the tiller, headed through the inlet. During the early morning hours Sam had worked on the engine of the smaller craft and it now ran quietly and smoothly. In a short time the boat reached the lagoon.

"It doesn't look haunted now in daylight," Doris remarked, as they gazed across the circular body of water, forest-bound to left and right of them. It was a little over half a mile in length and breadth. At the far side another narrow inlet led from the lagoon.

"The thief may be hiding up there!" Kim warned.

"I wonder," Louise mused, "if that exit connects with the inlet we saw blocked by the tree trunk."

Claude smiled. "Let's solve that mystery later," he said. "Right now I'd like to get out of the boat and explore this place on foot."

The Danas, who also were eager to start searching, were first out of the boat. They led the way through the high grass and among the trees. The sisters had gone only part way up the left side of the lagoon when Louise stopped, turned around, and said to the others tensely:

"Right ahead there's a little shack built on stilts. It's certainly well hidden from sight."

Excitedly the group ran forward and stared up at the one-room shack which had a long crude ladder propped against it.

When no one appeared in the open doorway, Claude called up, "Hello! Anybody at home?"

There was no answer. Louise announced that she was going to find out if someone was living in the shack and started up the ladder, with Jean close behind.

Claude, standing at the foot, looked worried. "Perhaps I should have gone first," he said, but the sisters reassured him.

"Do be careful!" Kim warned them from below. "Michael Fales, the thief, may be hiding up there!"

Undaunted, Louise reached the top of the ladder.

She peered inside the shack, then announced that no one was there.

"Somebody lives here, though," she stated, "and it looks as if he's been camping here for a long time."

She entered the shack, followed by Jean. Claude Cooper hurried up the rungs and joined them. At first glance there was no way to identify the resident of the house on stilts.

"Well, anyway, a man lives here," Jean said, seeing a pair of trousers and a jacket slung over a crude chair.

"These clothes wouldn't fit Michael Fales," Claude observed. Then he added excitedly, "But they would fit Captain Forsythe!"

CHAPTER XIX

A Skipper's Experiment

"Let's hunt for more clues!" Jean cried, and instantly she and Louise started a feverish search.

Almost at once Louise made a discovery. She picked up something from a roughly built table. "Here's a photograph. Claude, is this the *Sea Ghost* or is it the phantom ship?"

The young Englishman examined the picture carefully. "This was my family's boat," he said solemnly. "The ill-fated *Sea Ghost!*"

"Then this means," said Kim, "that Uncle Tracy does live here!"

"It certainly looks that way," Jean agreed.

"He must be nearby!" Kim urged an immediate search for the captain.

Quickly Claude and the girls climbed down the ladder of the shack. Automatically they turned toward the far side of the lagoon where they had seen the phantom ship.

Claude, in his eagerness to find Captain Forsythe, began to run and soon was some distance ahead of the others. Suddenly they heard him shout, *"Captain Forsythe!"*

Kim, Doris, and the Danas could scarcely believe their ears. The English girl, blinking back tears, began to race forward with her friends. When they drew near the shore of the lagoon, the girls halted abruptly.

There stood a handsome, erect man of fifty-five, wearing an English sailing captain's full uniform! He was wringing Claude's hand and embracing the young man affectionately.

"And, Captain Forsythe, this is little Kim Honeywell," Claude said, slipping his arm around the girl, who was overcome with emotion.

The captain stared at her a moment, then took her in his arms. "Little Kim—grown up now. I can't believe it."

"Oh, Uncle Tracy—it's so wonderful to see you!" Kim smiled joyously through her tears.

Stepping back, she introduced Louise, Jean, and Doris. Captain Forsythe gave each girl a hearty handshake and said how delighted he was to meet these friends of his niece and Claude. He was also happy to learn that his sister, too, was in Chincoteague.

Doris dimpled. "Captain Forsythe," she said, "we had a dreadful fright here last night. We saw a—a ghost ship. Can you tell us what's going on?"

"So it was you people who were here last night,"

Kim's uncle replied in surprise. "I did hear a boat. That's why I stopped my show," he added mysteriously.

Louise and Jean were looking intently at the captain. Finally Louise asked, "Do you have some device rigged up that causes a phantom ship to appear above the water?"

The sea captain nodded, and answered slowly, "I've kept my secret for several months, but I knew that eventually someone would find me out. I am glad that it turned out to be all of you."

"Please explain the mystery," Louise begged.

Captain Forsythe smiled and said, "Follow me."

He led them toward the spot where they had seen the phantom ship. When they reached the place the Danas and their friends blinked in amazement. A large, four-sided enclosure about thirty feet high, made of canvas and painted to imitate the woods, had been erected among the trees. One side faced the water.

As the visitors stared in astonishment, Captain Forsythe disappeared through a little doorway in the canvas. Within a few seconds the section which faced the lagoon began to drop forward. Even before it reached the water, the young people were exclaiming at what was revealed.

Before them was a full-rigged sailing vessel! Captain Forsythe stood on the deck.

"Come aboard and I'll tell you my story," he invited.

As the young people ascended the ship's ladder, they realized that the ship had only a thin hull and a bare deck below the sails.

"I constructed everything myself," Captain Forsythe stated.

"And I'm sure you painted the canvas camouflage yourself, too," said Claude. "I remember as a boy what wonderful pictures you made."

Captain Forsythe now looked at the Danas and Doris intently. Then he smiled again. "I have a feeling you already know part of the story from my niece and Claude, so I'll tell only the part they do not know."

Kim's uncle explained that for years he had been disturbed by the thought that although his memory was fine, it had continuously failed him on one point: He could remember little about what had happened the night of the *Sea Ghost's* fatal collision.

"It was very foggy and I had just glanced up at the sky when something hit me—I don't know what. Next thing I knew, I woke up in a hospital and heard we had rammed a freighter." The captain paused and bit his lip, then said, "I was accused of being responsible, and causing the death of several people I loved."

He went on, "About a year ago it occurred to me that if I could recreate the conditions prevailing on the night of the accident, perhaps my memory on the subject would come back. I decided to build this ship and rig it up to look like the lost *Sea Ghost*."

Proudly he pointed upward. "Those sheets are small, but every mainsail and jib are rigged to size. On foggy nights I come here with my uniform on. I gaze up into the sky and hope a miracle will happen."

Claude, putting his hand on the captain's shoulder, said, "We can help you fill in some of the details. Kim, I think you should do this."

Kim took hold of her uncle's hand. "Recently my father received word that one of your crew had made a deathbed confession. He had seen someone he thought was Michael Fales come up and strike you on the head. Anyway, it was Michael Fales who took over the running of the *Sea Ghost* and was really responsible for the accident."

"Fales!" Captain Forsythe cried out. Suddenly he clapped his other hand to his head. "I do remember one thing." He turned to Claude Cooper. "Was a large amount of money and securities found in my uniform after the accident?"

"No," Claude replied.

"Then Fales must have stolen all of it!" the captain shouted. "But everyone thought it went down with the ship. It didn't belong to me. A retired captain had asked me to transfer the currency and securities—his life's savings—from his own town to a bank in another place. The *Sea Ghost* was going to dock there."

Louise spoke up. "From what we know about Michael Fales, I'm sure that he did steal them. Also, his being a thief may account partly for his being in this region."

"He's around here?" Captain Forsythe exclaimed.

Louise told all they had learned. She concluded by saying she felt that Fales, after running away from England, had chosen Chincoteague as a place in which to hide in order to take the captain's prized pearl from him. "Do you still have it?" she asked.

Suddenly Kim's uncle began to laugh. "Well, on that account I fooled Fales. Just before the *Sea Ghost* started on her last voyage, I sold the pearl. Been living on the money it brought ever since. Now that I remember all about this, I'll reimburse my friend for his money and securities, unless perchance Scotland Yard can get it out of Fales."

Claude turned to the Danas. "Those deductions of yours were ripping," he said with a smile. "Exceedingly clever. And now, shall we start for Chincoteague?"

Captain Forsythe stared up into space for several seconds as if weighing the proposal carefully. Finally he said:

"I'm eager to see my sister, of course. But I don't want to give up my experiment here yet. I will never be completely happy until my own memory about the accident is completely restored. Combined with all you have told me, I think it will not be long now before I'll recall everything—perhaps even tonight. I expect there will be fog again. Please leave me here and come back later."

He gave the young people such a pleading smile that they could not refuse his request. Then the five companions left the deck of the ship and returned to the captain's shack.

He invited them to share lunch with him, and added, "No doubt you wonder where I get my supplies." He winked. "Twice a week, at night, I take my speedboat and meet a man out on the bay. He brings me everything I need. Queer kind of fellow, but I trust him implicitly. He spends most of his time hunting for medicinal herbs."

The Danas and their friends were startled by this disclosure, and Jean asked, "Does this man live on Mills Island and is his name Kurt Welch?"

It was now the captain's turn to look surprised. Jean told him about the rescue of the irascible Welch from the pit. "Maybe the night he spent in it was when he was supposed to meet you, and that upset him," she added.

Captain Forsythe chuckled. "Welch didn't tell me about it—he doesn't talk much. But it's true he failed to meet me—never bothered to explain why."

At that moment the group heard approaching footsteps and presently Sam Everett, Ken, and

Chris came into view. Their mud-spattered boots indicated they had walked in from the bay. Captain Forsythe greeted his old acquaintance, then was introduced to the two boys. Ken and Chris told the girls that Ronny had stayed behind to guard their digging site.

"So you're looking for treasure, eh?" Captain Forsythe's eyes gleamed. "For years I hoped to find that pirate hoard, and even took a try at it. But I never had any luck."

Ken confessed that except for the brass earring he had found, the boys had had no success, either. "But we're not giving up," he stated.

Sam Everett had carried the picnic lunch from the cruiser. Kim gaily said, "Uncle Tracy, please be our guest."

Everyone sat down among the sweet-smelling pine trees to enjoy the tasty chicken sandwiches, fruit, and cake. There were so many stories to exchange that the afternoon quickly passed.

"I think we should go now," Doris spoke up, and her friends agreed.

They said good-by to Captain Forsythe and told him that they would return the next day and bring Mrs. Honeywell with them. The boys started their hike back to the bay. Sam and the girls took the dinghy out of the inlet. The motor was kept throttled, so the little boat would not get too far ahead of the trekkers.

As they reached the cruiser, Louise looked very pensive. When Jean asked what was on her mind, her sister said, "I don't know how the rest of you feel about leaving here, but I'm against it. We know now that Michael Fales hasn't located your uncle, Kim. But he or some spy of his may have trailed us here today."

"That's right." Jean nodded gravely. "Michael Fales may come to the lagoon after dark and try to harm the captain again."

Kim uttered a cry of dismay and Claude drew in his breath. Both declared that they wished to remain.

"I think we should all go back and do our best to protect Captain Forsythe," Louise went on. "We won't let him know we're around, of course, so he can continue his experiment undisturbed."

Ken and Chris liked the idea, and offered to act as guards for the sea captain. Claude promptly said he would join them, and Sam Everett declared he would not be left out.

"You young ladies can watch from the other side of the lagoon," the pilot added.

The Danas would have preferred being right on hand to help guard the captain, but Sam Everett would not agree to this. "We men will do that."

Jean reminded the others that Kim's uncle would hear the dinghy's engine. "So let's use the oars this time."

"If you're going to do that, you'd better get started," Sam Everett urged.

Dusk, accompanied by fog, had fallen by the time the group had quietly returned to the lagoon for their secret vigil. The girls remained in the dinghy just beyond the inlet, while Sam Everett and the boys disappeared in the mist. The strong beam from the Assateague lighthouse was already at work and the girls hoped it would not reveal their presence to the captain.

They sat in silence for some time, staring ahead expectantly for the phantom ship to emerge. Suddenly the main and fore skysails appeared through the mist. Little by little, as the painted tree canvas was lowered, the rest of the rigging appeared, then the deck and a little bit of the hull. The lower part of the hull was obscured, thus making it seem as if the ghostly ship were suspended in mid-air.

Captain Forsythe's tall figure could be seen standing aboard. He was gazing upward.

At this instant the girls heard the motor of a speedboat start up. They were thunderstruck. Had the boys turned on the motor of the captain's speedboat? Or—had someone else been hiding in the lagoon? Before they could come to any conclusion, the four girls heard a splintering crash.

"Oh dear, what happened?" Doris cried out.

At this instant the scene was illuminated once more by the lighthouse beam. To the girls' horror, they could see that a speedboat had rammed the phantom ship, tearing apart its thin hull. The masts were toppling, carrying the sails to the deck.

In panic, Kim cried out, "Oh, Uncle Tracy! Uncle Tracy! Where are you?"

Captain Forsythe was no longer standing on the deck. Had he been thrown down and badly injured?

CHAPTER XX

Pieces of Eight

THE FOUR girls leaped from the dinghy as if they had been catapulted from it. When the beam from the Assateague lighthouse illuminated the scene of the wrecked ghost ship, they could make out the figures of Sam Everett and the three boys dashing into the water. They were chasing a man who apparently had jumped from the speedboat and was trying to escape.

"It's Jake Maxwell!" the girls heard Sam Everett yell. "Don't let him get away, fellows!"

By the time the Danas, Doris, and Kim arrived, the prisoner was being brought ashore. It took little persuasion to get Maxwell to make a full confession. He admitted being an accomplice of a man from London named Smith, but instead of being contrite he seemed pleased about the role.

"I was a right smart lookout for Smith," Maxwell bragged. "Told him where the captain was, and rigged up a log to close the inlet."

When asked about the damage to the sailing

vessel he had caused a few minutes before, he replied, "I don't know what it's all about. Late this afternoon I met Smith out in the bay. He told me what to do—promised he'd pay me well for the job."

"If he pays you at all," Claude told the prisoner icily, "it will be with money he stole in England. I don't believe you didn't know that. Anyhow, he's wanted by the police on both sides of the Atlantic. Where is he now?"

"He hides on Mills Island."

While this conversation was going on, the Danas, with Kim and Doris, were crawling up onto the ruined phantom ship. Ahead, almost completely covered by spars and tangled sails, lay Captain Forsythe, unconscious. It was impossible for the girls to rescue the man, with the deck tilted at a precarious angle.

"Ken! Chris!" Jean shouted over the railing. "We need help. Captain Forsythe must be carried down."

While Sam Everett and Claude Cooper kept tight hold of their prisoner, the two boys made their way to the captain. Lifting the debris aside, they placed their arms under the captain's shoulders and carefully raised him up. Louise and Jean grasped his ankles, and, moving at a snail's pace, the four were finally able to get the captain to solid ground.

"We'd better take him to the shack," Louise suggested.

Kim wanted to help, but she had been so unnerved by what had happened that her strength had ebbed completely. Doris supported the trembling girl as they walked to the shack.

"I am not sure we can get the captain up—that ladder doesn't look strong enough," said Ken, gazing upward.

At that moment their burden stirred. His bearers laid him gently on the ground and a few moments later he opened his eyes.

"I saw a flashlight in the shack," said Jean. "I'll get it." She went up the ladder as nimbly as a monkey and soon brought back the flashlight.

By this time Captain Forsythe had raised himself on one elbow. He looked about him dazedly for a few seconds, then his mind seemed to clear.

"Are you all right, Uncle Tracy?" Kim asked solicitously. She was kneeling beside him.

The captain blinked, then the trace of a smile crossed his face. "Yes, my dear. I'm fit as a fiddle. What's more, I can remember everything now." His eyes narrowed. "It *was* Michael Fales who sneaked up and hit me on the head aboard the *Sea Ghost!* He muttered a few words. I recognized that voice! Fales was always jealous of my position and vowed he'd take it away from me."

"There was never any chance of that!" Claude spoke up, fire in his eyes.

Captain Forsythe went on, "I expect Fales hoped to make it seem as if I'd knocked myself out by falling. He was going to bring the *Sea Ghost* safely through the fog and get all the credit. But his scheme didn't work. Mike Fales took over but did a bad job of navigating—and actually caused the accident."

"And ahead of that, he took the money and securities from you," Claude deduced.

Captain Forsythe now stood up, and declared he was ready to testify against Michael Fales at any time. Louise explained the recent accident and pointed out Jake Maxwell.

The captain stared at the prisoner in disgust a couple of seconds, then he laughed dryly. "You know, that scoundrel Fales really did me a good turn—having me knocked out a second time. It restored that part of my memory which he hoped was dead forever."

"And now let's hurry to Chincoteague," Kim urged. "What a surprise we'll have for Mother!"

"Not so fast, young lady," Captain Forsythe said. "I want to see my sister, but there's some dunnage in the shack I can't leave here unguarded. It'll take time to pack. Pretty foggy weather, too. How about all of you spending the night here and we'll set sail in the morning?"

Kim was reluctant to leave her uncle now that she had found him and readily agreed to stay, if word could be sent to Mrs. Honeywell.

"And to my parents, too," Doris added.

Jean said to Chris, "How about your short-wave

two-way radio? And we ought to notify the police, anyway."

"Good idea," Sam Everett said, "and tell 'em I aim to get this prisoner of ours to Chincoteague as soon as possible."

Chris soon made contact with the law officers, who promised to start an immediate search on Mills. Also, they would notify Mr. and Mrs. Harland and Mrs. Honeywell of the girls' plans.

Jake Maxwell was securely tied before Sam Everett set off with him. He said that they would go on foot to the cruiser and leave the dinghy and speedboat behind. It was now revealed that the boat Maxwell had used to ram the ship was Captain Forsythe's!

"I didn't hurt it much," Jake grunted as he was marched off.

Captain Forsythe said that the girls could bunk in the shack. The three boys and he would sleep on the ground.

In the morning the young people helped the captain pack his belongings, and stow them in his speedboat, which fortunately was still afloat and in running condition.

When everyone was ready to leave, Ken asked, "Can somebody take Chris and me back to Ronny?"

It was decided that Kim and Claude would go with Captain Forsythe in his speedboat, while the Danas and Doris would head north with the boys.

The dinghy left first, with its occupants waving good-by to the English trio.

"Oh, I just can't believe the mystery of Captain Forsythe is solved!" Doris said as they proceeded.

Ken grinned. "Your mystery may be solved, but ours isn't. That pirate treasure is still underground. How about you girls lending a hand again and helping us find it?"

"I suppose," Jean began, looking at Chris with mischief in her eyes, "that the only way I'll ever get that bracelet made of pieces of eight is to dig them up myself!"

"Is that so?" Chris flung back. "Just for that I'll show you!"

When the dinghy reached Ronny, he looked exceedingly relieved to see them. "Boy, I thought maybe all of you were adrift in a boat out on the ocean. Where've you been?"

As the story was unfolded to him, Ronny's eyes bulged. "You might know I'd miss all the excitement," he said. "But then, I've had a little of my own. Look here!"

He walked into the tent, reached down, and came back with handfuls of Spanish doubloons.

"Wow!" Chris exclaimed. "Did you dig these up?"

"Nobody else," his chum answered. "The place is loaded with gold!"

"What're we waiting for!" Ken exclaimed.

The six young people decided, because of the

shortage of tools, to work in pairs. The couples continued to deepen and enlarge the holes already made. Presently Jean and Chris came upon enough pieces of eight for the promised bracelet.

"What did I tell you?" Chris grinned.

Just then they heard a loud whoop from Louise and Ken, who stepped out of a hole to display a small metal chest. The other two couples rushed to their sides and watched as the ancient lock was broken off and the cover raised.

"A fortune!" Doris cried out.

Inside the chest were rings, necklaces, bracelets, and pins, all set with precious stones.

"That old pirate really made a haul!" Ronny remarked. "Say, the United States government certainly won't mind getting their share of this!"

Each piece was lifted out and examined, then returned, and the lid closed. Elated by their find, the treasure seekers set the chest of jewels off to one side near the woods and continued digging.

It was only a few minutes before Ronny cried out, "Doris and I have found another chest!"

The group gathered once more above ground and opened the second chest. This one contained ancient pistols, swords, and daggers. The boys were intrigued, and examined them closely.

Louise, not so interested, had raised her eyes toward the woods. The next second she screamed. "I just saw Michael Fales! He—he has stolen our chest of jewels!"

The thief could be seen dashing off among the trees. Quickly Louise suggested that Doris and Ronny stay to guard the other treasures, then urged, "Come on, Jean! Ken! Chris!"

The pursuit began, with Fales dodging in and out among the trees and bushes. The Danas were afraid he might be heading for a boat and would take off in it before they could capture him. Running as fast as possible, the four were having no luck trying to overtake the fugitive.

Suddenly Jean exclaimed, "Listen!" The sounds of galloping ponies came closer and closer. The next moment a band of the wild animals pounded toward Michael Fales and almost surrounded him.

"They've cut off his escape!" Louise cried excitedly.

Fales had had no choice but to stop. The ponies, seeing him, halted and stared. Then they turned their backs on him and ran off.

The delay proved to be costly for Michael Fales. Ken and Chris dashed forward and grabbed him. Louise and Jean arrived a moment later. The prisoner glared at them all, then muttered, "All right. You blokes got me. What do you want to know?"

Louise and Jean lost no time in firing questions at the captured thief. They learned that Michael Fales had two henchmen in the Chincoteague area —Jake Maxwell and a Maryland resident who called himself Scribner. The trio had engineered various schemes to keep the Danas from solving the mystery of Captain Forsythe's whereabouts.

One had phoned the fake message to the hotel that Sam Everett could not take the group out in his boat. Scribner had invented the story of Captain Forsythe being on the yacht. Other episodes, figured out previously by the Danas and Captain Forsythe, as well as Kim, Claude, and Doris, proved to be correct. It was he who had dropped the English coin on Pirate Island.

Ken had already retrieved the chest of jewels from the thief. Now Fales was marched ahead of the group and led to the beach, where Doris and Ronny expressed their relief that at last the wanted lawbreaker would be turned over to the police.

Michael Fales's hands were tied behind his back, his ankles were bound together, and he was put in a spot where he could be watched every moment. The sleuthing treasure hunters decided it best to wait for Sam Everett to come and take all of them, their valuable finds, and equipment back to town.

Presently Doris sang out, "Here he comes now!"

The cruiser pulled up to the beach. On it were Mr. and Mrs. Harland, Mrs. Honeywell, Captain Forsythe, and Kim and Claude. All came ashore and listened in amazement to the conclusion of the mystery and the treasure hunt's rewarding results.

Meanwhile, Captain Forsythe was looking with

icy contempt at Michael Fales. The prisoner glared malevolently at his former captain for one second, then lowered his eyes to the ground.

Mrs. Honeywell, seeing this, said, "I suggest we not spoil the joyful ending to our search for my brother. Let the police handle the prisoner. Kim and I are exceedingly happy at the outcome. Louise and Jean and Doris, we shall always owe you a debt of gratitude."

Kim smiled at the trio. "If I ever have another mystery to be solved, I'm coming to the three best American detectives I know!"

Louise, Jean, and Doris blushed at the praise.

The Danas suddenly realized they had no further sleuthing to do. But in a short time they were to find themselves confronted with another case, *Mystery of the Bamboo Bird*.

Now they merely smiled, giving full credit to the part Sam Everett, Nat Steelman, and Mr. and Mrs. Wolfe had played in solving the story of the haunted lagoon.

Captain Forsythe added his thanks also. "And now Claude has a special announcement to make."

With a sweep of his hand, the young Englishman said, "I'm going to have a new model of the old *Sea Ghost* built. Captain Forsythe will skipper her. I hereby extend an invitation that my first guests be all you kind American friends!"